PUFFI...

DAN

Dan Lunn has the perfect family – in his head: a handsome father, an attractive mother, a lively small sister. But in reality there's his pious grandfather, neurotic mother and absent, alcoholic father. When, eventually, his mother runs away with a stranger, Dan is thrown on to the charity of his relatives, an unhappy experience which makes him run away too. He hides in the murky streets of the Jungle, the squalid part of town, and there he is befriended by Leo who introduces him to his 'family'. However, they're not the warm and affectionate family for which Dan craves, and despite plausible explanations, he can't believe that what they are doing is right.

How Dan comes to discover the father he has never known and to find the love and security he most needs makes a rich and appealing story.

Other books by John Rowe Townsend published in Puffins are: *Gumbles' Yard*, *Hell's Edge* and *The Islanders*. And in Puffin Plus: *Noah's Castle*, *A Foreign Affair* and *The Intruder*.

JOHN ROWE TOWNSEND

Dan Alone

PUFFIN BOOKS

Puffin Books, Penguin Books Ltd, Harmondsworth, Middlesex, England
Viking Penguin Inc., 40 West 23rd Street, New York, New York 10010, U.S.A.
Penguin Books Australia Ltd, Ringwood, Victoria, Australia
Penguin Books Canada Ltd, 2801 John Street, Markham, Ontario, Canada L3R 1B4
Penguin Books (N.Z.) Ltd, 182–190 Wairau Road, Auckland 10, New Zealand

First published by Kestrel Books 1983
Published in Puffin Books 1985

Made and printed in Great Britain by
Richard Clay (The Chaucer Press) Ltd,
Bungay, Suffolk
Filmset in Palatino

CHAPTER 1

Dan Lunn walked down City Hill in a crowd of one. His eyes had a faraway look, his lips moved soundlessly from time to time, and occasionally he smiled at some invisible person. He didn't watch where he was going. Twice he bumped into people. A woman protested mildly and a man swore at him, but Dan didn't hear them. He noticed nobody, and apart from the two he bumped into, nobody noticed him.

He was not a noticeable boy. At eleven he was skinny, narrow-faced and pale, with brown eyes and straight dark hair. He wore a flat cap with a peak, a long grey jersey pulled well down, and shorts that half-covered his knobbly knees. His stick-like calves disappeared into black ankle-boots, so stout and emphatic that they seemed to be carrying him around rather than he them.

Under the peaked cap, a family chattered away: an imaginary family. Its members were a handsome father, an attractive mother, a bright, lively small sister, and Dan himself. To Dan this family was more real than the people around him, and he spent a lot of time with it. It was the reason why he was often oblivious to his actual surroundings.

That afternoon, however, he had real-life duties. In his pocket, clutched in a hand for extra security, were a silver shilling and four large copper pennies. Dan was on an errand for his grandfather. From time to time he brought himself down to earth and reminded himself of what he had to buy: a half-pound of butter and a quarter of fivepenny tea. He was to get them from Bradshaws and nowhere else.

Bradshaws were a long way down the hill from Grandpa's house. Grandpa lived near the top, in the Marigolds. The Marigolds were Marigold Street, Marigold Grove, Marigold Mount, Marigold Way, Marigold Avenue, Marigold Hill and Marigold Terrace. Similar clusters of streets, named after other flowers, sprawled all over City Hill. Through the middle of them ran a main road, and up and down the main road ran the tall two-decker tramcar. The tramcar groaned painfully upward, on its way to the outer suburbs, then went into reverse and came wailing and clanging back into town at twice the speed.

Up was good, down was bad. The topmost streets of City Hill were the Chrysanthemums, which were superior to all others. Then came the Marigolds; then the Primroses, Lilies and Daisies. All these were respectable. Doorsteps were scoured, children decently dressed, front parlours icy with propriety. Farther down, among the Roses and Violets, deterioration set in, with shabby curtains and women who wore curlers in the streets. And farther down still came the Orchids and Camellias and Mimosas of the Jungle, where neglect was general. A window might stay broken for weeks or be stuffed with newspapers, though the pale Jewish glazier was always around and would have mended it for ninepence.

The Jungle was the lowest place of all, alarming to those higher up. When he was very small, Dan had thought of Heaven as somewhere uphill beyond the Chrysanthemums, and Hell as lying in the Jungle's black crumbling depths. Bradshaws the grocers were close to the Jungle but not of it. There was an air of uphill respectability about them.

'A half-pound of butter and a quarter of fivepenny tea,' said Dan to stout Mrs Bradshaw, getting his order

6

right and adding, by way of credentials, 'It's for Mr Purvis. My grandpa.'

'And how *is* Mr Purvis?' Mrs Bradshaw asked. She didn't wait for a reply, but went straight on. 'A fine man, your Grandpa. I don't know what they'd do without him at the Chapel.' She added, as a further testimonial, 'Always pays cash, too.'

It never surprised Dan to hear his grandfather praised. Grandpa, who had recently retired from work, was known all over the Hill and highly regarded by most. He was round-faced, with a fringe of white hair and steel-rimmed spectacles. He was a mild, kind, accommodating man in any matter except religion, on which he was stern and unyielding. Grandpa had a fierce hatred of Jews and Catholics, and a strong dislike for any church that went in for more ceremony than his own austere sect. Besides being a pillar of the Chapel, he was fruitful in good works and ready with a Biblical quotation for any emergency.

'Your grandfather's a saint,' a neighbour had said to Dan, only a week or two previously. Dan knew it, and Grandpa knew it himself. It was a privilege to live so close to a saint, but it was often an ordeal. Wickedness lay in wait for Dan. So small a failure could be sinful. An act of unkindness, forgetfulness or momentary greed would bring the clouds to Grandpa's brow. To Grandpa, and doubtless to God, the small sins of small boys were no laughing matter.

Grandpa was a widower. He had two daughters. The elder was Dan's Aunt Verity, a plain and virtuous woman who wore pebble-lensed spectacles. At the age of thirty, Aunt Verity had married a salesman of dog-biscuits, Uncle Bert. Unwilling to compete with Grandpa's formidable piety, Uncle Bert kept at a respect-ful distance. He and Aunt Verity had one son: large, pale Basil, two years older than Dan. Dan feared and hated Basil.

The other daughter was Mum. Dan lived with Mum in Daisy Mount. Mum worked in a city store until half-past five, which was why Dan always went to Grandpa's house after school. This afternoon, Dan's route back to Grandpa's from the grocers' would take him past the corner of Daisy Mount, but he wouldn't even look in the direction of his own house. It was Thursday, and he knew, though Grandpa didn't, that on Thursdays Mum often got home early. She would probably be in the house now. But she wouldn't want to see Dan before the usual time, because she wouldn't be alone there. Uncle Alec would be with her.

Mum was pale, pretty, round-faced and dark-haired, childishly small and thin. She had been married young and in haste, and was still only twenty-nine. Herself a late and unexpected child, she had been Grandpa's joy: his consolation over many years for the loss of his wife. She and Grandpa were child and parent still. Just lately, a coolness had come between them, but until then she had always taken her problems to Grandpa and he had told her what to do about them.

One of her problems was Jack Lunn, Dan's dad. Jack turned up at Daisy Mount two or three times a year. If sober, he would be asking for money. If drunk, he would ask for money when he sobered up. With Grandpa's help, Mum always managed to find some money for him. Then he would disappear again. Mum never referred to Jack as her husband or as Dan's father. Neither she nor Grandpa referred to him at all if they could help it. If they did have to mention him, they always spoke of him by his full name, Jack Lunn.

And now, since six months ago, there was Uncle Alec, who wasn't a real uncle. He came to see Mum on Thursday afternoons and sometimes at weekends as well. If he appeared at the weekend, Dan would be sent out of the house. On such occasions, Uncle Alec would give Dan a penny, twopence, or perhaps even threepence to spend; but Dan didn't like him. Dan had been told by Mum that he was not to mention Uncle Alec to Grandpa; and he would not have done so anyway. He knew without being told what Grandpa would have thought.

Today, clutching his butter and tea in a brown paper bag, Dan passed the end of Daisy Mount without a glance or a conscious thought. He had retreated once more into his imaginary world. In his mind was a father who was nothing like either Jack Lunn or Uncle Alec: a father who was tall and broad-shouldered and curly-haired and cheerful and reliable. There was a small sister, beautiful and adoring, who looked up to Dan as her hero. There was Mum, too: his actual Mum, but changed, for now she was calm and happy and fulfilled, with her husband and children around her.

A particular scene was printed on Dan's mind, to be returned to again and again, like a photograph. The little sister was swinging between the two parents, holding a hand of each and smiling up at them alternately. The three of them were united and affectionate and *his*. Because Jack Lunn was hardly ever around and was so much despised by Mum and Grandpa, Dan had allowed his imagination to provide a new model father in Jack's place. But he had never actually suspected that Jack was not his real dad.

Dan pulled himself back into the real world as he approached Grandpa's house in Marigold Grove. It was a cold day in March, with a hint of rain on the wind. As usual Dan went to the back door, which opened straight into the kitchen. Facing each other across the kitchen table were Grandpa and his neighbour Hilda Selby. They were deep in conversation. Dan had heard their voices – Hilda's clear and penetrating, Grandpa's mild and low – as he came through the back yard. They broke off as he entered, seeming slightly disconcerted.

9

'You're soon back, Daniel,' said Grandpa. He didn't sound altogether pleased.

'There, there, he doesn't *always* dawdle,' said Hilda brightly. 'Do you, Dan dear?' She smiled sweetly at him. Dan didn't respond.

Grandpa and Hilda had become very friendly in the last year or so. Their friendship wasn't at all like that of Mum and Uncle Alec. It had never caused a breath of scandal. The whole congregation of the Chapel knew about it, and everyone approved: everyone, that is, except Mum, who was bitterly jealous of Hilda.

Hilda was a mature widow, plump in face and figure yet oddly small-eyed and small-mouthed. She had devoted her youth to looking after ailing parents and in early middle age had found a husband, only to lose him through a fatal accident at work within a year of the marriage. Now she was alone in the world. It was understood that she had a small private income. She had a true though strident voice which dominated the Chapel choir, and in addition she deputized at the harmonium. Sometimes of an evening she came to Grandpa's house and played hymns on the ancient upright piano in his front room, while Grandpa sang beside her in a passable baritone and both of them rejoiced in a relationship which must surely be pleasing in the sight of God.

Grandpa reached out absently for Dan's brown-paper package. Obviously he had something on his mind. 'Mrs Selby and I have matters to discuss,' he said eventually, 'which are not the business of a child. You may go into the front room, Daniel, and read a book until it is time for you to go home.'

Dan didn't mind that. He would rather go into the parlour and read a book than make polite conversation with Hilda, who, for all her sweetness to him, didn't really like children and didn't know how to get on with them.

10

The parlour was a gloomy room, but Dan was used to it. Its main feature was a Lord's Prayer which Grandpa had cut out of satinwood in fretwork. It was two feet wide and three feet high, mounted on dark blue plush, framed under glass, and hung on the wall. Grandpa had designed it himself, and the making of it had taken three years of his leisure time. It had Gothic lettering surrounded by marvellously convoluted scrolls and flourishes.

As he neared the end of his task, Grandpa's fretsaw had slipped and taken the middle out of the final *e* in 'for ever and ever'. He was not dismayed, and often pointed to this flaw as demonstrating the imperfection of all human achievement. 'Only that which God does is perfect,' he used to say.

Dan looked for the book he'd started reading the previous week. Grandpa's books had been carefully preserved from his own Victorian childhood. Most were Sunday School prizes for regular attendance, good conduct, or knowledge of the Scriptures. There were stories in which children of astonishing virtue suffered dreadful injustice in silence. There were others in which children strayed from the straight and narrow path but were brought back to it repentant, or in which radiantly saintly children acted as beacons of light for erring adults. In all of these stories, life was real and earnest; poverty and hunger were commonplace, families were stalked by the Demon Drink, death and damnation were ever-present possibilities. They had for Dan a fearful fascination.

The one he was reading now was about two waifs on the streets of London who befriended an apparently poor old man, found him to be a rich miser, converted him to religion and benevolence, and discovered that he was their long-lost great-uncle. The old gentleman died soon afterwards, having survived just long enough to

11

regret his misspent life and alter his will in the children's favour.

Dan was halfway through the last chapter – a lengthy account of the old man's beautiful and repentant death-bed – when he found it necessary to go to the bathroom. And as he crossed the hallway on his way back to the parlour, Hilda Selby's penetrating voice came clearly to him from the kitchen.

'Poor little lad!' she was saying to Grandpa. 'So he really thinks Jack Lunn is his father!'

CHAPTER 2

Dan stood unmoving for a few seconds, his mind benumbed. Although in his imagination he'd been ready enough to replace Jack Lunn as his father, the sudden indication that Jack was no such thing was shattering. As he stood, he heard Grandpa's quieter voice, saying anxiously, 'Ssssh! Hilda! He's in the next room!'

And Dan fled. He didn't actually decide to go; his legs ran away with him. He flung himself out through Grandpa's front door and raced along Marigold Grove, running blindly. His feet took him the usual way: through the Marigolds, down the main road for a hundred yards, past the tram stop and half a dozen pairs of corner shops, and across the Daisies to the house where he and Mum lived.

Arriving in Daisy Mount, he slowed down. Though it was now almost his usual time for getting home, there was just a chance that Uncle Alec would still be there. He went round through the yard and quietly up to the back door. There was no sound from inside and no light visible. But the key wasn't under the brick where it was kept when there was nobody in the house. Mum must be there. He pushed the door gently open and went in.

She was in the living-room, alone, sitting in her usual armchair, so quiet and motionless that he could easily have failed to see her.

Dan stood in front of her, panting. He wanted to burst out with a question. But his stammer came upon him, and the words wouldn't come. His mouth opened and closed uselessly.

'Well!' she said. 'What you looking like that for?'

The smell of cigarette-smoke was in the air, and telltale threads of smoke curled between her fingers. Instinctively she'd held the cigarette out of sight, but now she brought it out defiantly.

Dan still couldn't get his question out. Mum thought it was the cigarette that was on his mind. It was rare for him to find her smoking. She concealed it on account of Grandpa. Grandpa disapproved of smoking, especially by women and above all by Mum.

'It's only a Woodbine now and then,' she said. 'No need for your Grandpa to know. He's so old-fashioned. After all, it *is* 1922!' She smiled sideways at Dan, inviting him to conspire with her.

Then it came out, in a rapid rush of words.

'Jack Lunn isn't my dad,' he said. '*Who is*?'

His mother, startled, choked on the cigarette-smoke. She stubbed out what was left of the Woodbine and demanded sharply, 'Who told you that?'

Dan stepped back a pace. He opened his mouth, but no answer came out. Mum got up and put her hands on his shoulders. She was hardly taller than he was.

'Go on. Who told you?' And then, 'Where've you been? At Grandpa's?'

Dan nodded.

'But you're not going to say your Grandpa told you that?'

Dan shook his head. 'No. I heard Mrs S-s-selby say . . .' His voice faltered.

'That woman! What did she say? Come on now, out with it!'

Dan's stammer was slight, but it always got worse under stress. Once again he couldn't speak. Mum pressed her fingers into his shoulders.

'Tell me what Mrs Selby said!'

'She said, "P-p-p . . ."' Dan swallowed and started again. 'She said, "Poor little lad, he thinks Jack Lunn is his father!"'

'He told her!' Mum said in a tone of bitter outrage. 'He *told* her! *Her*!'

She dropped her hands from Dan's shoulders, sat down again in the big armchair that seemed to surround her, and was silent. Dan, recovering voice and initiative, went in to the attack.

'Who *is* my dad?' he asked again.

There was another silence. Dan repeated the question. Mum took another Woodbine from the little paper packet of five. Her hand shook slightly as she lit it. Then she said thoughtfully, 'You don't know Jack Lunn isn't your dad. You don't know anything about it. You don't have to listen to what Hilda Selby says. It wasn't meant for your ears anyway. So just you be quiet about it. It's none of your business.'

'It *is* my business. My dad's my business. Everybody's dad's their business.'

'Jack Lunn's all the dad you have. No more use to you than he is to me, I dare say, but I married him and that makes him your dad. Now go away and stop bothering me.'

'But I have a real dad, haven't I?'

No answer.

14

'Haven't I?'

No answer.

'Mum, tell me. I want to know. Who's my real dad? Is he alive? *Where* is he? Mum. *Mum!*'

Mum flicked the ash off the Woodbine. She said, slowly, 'I suppose you had to know some time. No, Jack Lunn's not your dad really. But his name's on your birth certificate, so he might as well be. You haven't any other.'

'I have, I must have. He *is* alive, isn't he? He must be somewhere. I know he's somewhere.'

'You don't know anything of the sort. Lots of children don't have dads. Lots of dads got killed in the Great War. Look at the Stanleys. There's five of them and no dad. He was killed on the Western Front, was Harold Stanley. And Mrs Stanley has a hard time bringing them up, I can tell you. Compared with the Stanleys, you're well off, Dan Lunn. You don't know you're born.'

'*My* dad wasn't killed in the war,' said Dan, knowing it from her voice. '*My* dad's not dead. Where is he?'

She was beginning to break down.

'No, he's not dead,' she said. 'Though he might as well be. There's times when I wish he was, and when I wish *I* was, too. You've no business asking me such things. And all through *her*, too. It upsets me, it does really.' She was weeping now. 'You ought not to be here, Daniel! You oughtn't ever to have been born. You was begun in sin and you came into the world in sin, and how can I forget it? Oh, Dan, Dan!' The Woodbine fell to the linoleum, and Mum stamped on it with vicious accuracy. Then she had her arms round her son. 'I'll never forget your Grandpa's face when I told him. I thought it would kill him!'

Dan was silent now. Mum hardly ever embraced him. He could feel her tears on his own cheek.

'He took it like the saint he is,' Mum said. 'He's

forgiven me, though he can't forget. How *could* he forget, any more than I can? Anyway, he made sure you'd have a name. Jack Lunn wouldn't have married me without the house, and it was your Grandpa's money that bought the house. It cost him most of what he had. Oh, your poor Grandpa, the grief I brought him!'

Mum wept again. 'And he didn't know Jack would turn out so badly. That was more sorrow for him. All the same, he shouldn't have told that Hilda Selby. She must have wormed it out of him, she's just the type. I shall go round there and give her a piece of my mind, I shall really and no mistake.'

She released Dan. 'And listen to me, Dan Lunn. You will not, you will never, you will *never ever*, say anything about it to any living soul, you understand? It's bad enough being married to Jack Lunn, but at least I *am* married, and nobody can say I'm not.'

'What's my real dad's name?' Dan asked.

'That,' said Mum, 'I am not telling you and never will, not till you're grown-up and maybe not then. Maybe not till he's dead. He might die, he was never strong, he wasn't fit for the Army.'

She was crying again. A new question came to Dan's lips. He didn't know how it got there. It came out unconsidered.

'Did you love him?' he asked.

He jumped back hastily but wasn't quick enough. His mother flew at him, slapping him first on one cheek and then on the other in a burst of fury. Then she slumped again into the chair, sobbing noisily. Dan stood where he was, cheeks red from the slap, not knowing what to say or do.

'Don't look at me like that!' she cried. 'Stop punishing me!' She turned her eyes to the ceiling. 'Oh God, stop punishing me!'

CHAPTER 3

Mum dried her eyes, powdered her face, and put on her little velour hat. She wiped Dan's eyes, too, and told him to blow his nose and fetch his cap and fasten all his buttons and pull up his stockings.

'We're going round to your Grandpa's this minute,' she said. 'And I hope she's still there. I'm going to have it out with them both.'

'I don't want to come,' said Dan.

'Well, you're *going* to come. What if she was to deny it? I wouldn't put anything past that woman.' And then, suspiciously, 'It *is* the truth you've been telling me, Dan? Look at me. Look straight at me. It is the truth, isn't it, and not wicked lies?'

'It's true,' said Dan miserably.

'Well then, come on. Let's get it over and done with. You needn't think I'm going to enjoy it.'

Mum took Dan by the hand and stalked through the streets, half a pace ahead. She held him firmly and with good reason, because he'd have wriggled out of her grip and run away if he could. Halfway through the Marigolds, she came to a stop. Approaching them along the pavement was the tall figure of the Jewish glazier.

Everyone in the district knew the glazier. The younger children were afraid of him. He wore an ancient, rusty, black frock-coat, and his boots were broken. He had a pale, bearded face and deep, dark eyes, and was sometimes referred to as Jesus Christ; but once, when some big boys had thrown stones and had smashed the glass in the wooden frame he always carried, he had shaken

17

his fist and shouted at them in a most un-Christlike manner before bending to pick broken glass out of the gutter.

Today he saw Mum and Dan coming, and crossed the road to avoid them.

'Don't you ever speak to him, Dan Lunn!' said Mum as she got back into her stride; but Dan didn't need the warning. He would never have spoken to the glazier.

As they neared Marigold Grove, Mum's pace increased. Her face was white, and not only with face-powder. Her lips moved as she rehearsed what she was going to say.

She marched up to Grandpa's front door and opened it without knocking. She stood for a moment in the hall-way, listening for voices. They came from the parlour now, and Mum pushed Dan into it ahead of her. It was a room some twelve feet square, dominated by two or three pieces of heavy rosewood furniture and the upright piano. The Lord's Prayer hung on one wall; on another was a monochrome reproduction of a painting called 'The Light of the World'. The fireplace was screened off, but a gas fire flickered pinkly in front of it. The room wasn't cold, yet felt it; Grandpa's parlour always felt cold.

Grandpa and Hilda Selby were sitting side by side on the sofa, poring over an album. There was a slightly guilty look on their faces, almost as if they'd been found holding hands. Mum stood in front of them, gripping Dan by the wrist so tightly that it hurt.

'What have you been telling this boy, Hilda Selby?' she demanded.

Grandpa and Hilda, startled, rose together from the sofa. Hilda opened her mouth and closed it again with-out speaking. A huge, slow blush spread over her cheeks. Grandpa's mild round face grew stern. He had a remarkable capacity for sternness; often it seemed to

18

those around him as if some more awesome, divine displeasure spoke through him.

'Prue,' he said. 'Prudence Lunn. Do you know where you are? You are in your father's house. You don't shout like that here.'

Though the rebuke was not directed at Dan, it made him feel fear in the pit of his stomach. But it didn't stop Mum. She'd been working up to an outburst, and had impetus enough to carry her over the obstacle of Grandpa's disapproval.

'She's told him Jack Lunn isn't his dad!' she proclaimed.

There was a silence which Dan broke with a murmur of dissent.

'She didn't tell me, I overheard.'

'That makes it worse!' Mum faced Grandpa in fury. 'You told *her*, and she let it drop. She *would*! Who else will she be telling, I'd like to know?'

Grandpa spoke very quietly. 'Let the boy go, Prue,' he instructed.

'He'll run away if I do.'

'No, he will not. Daniel, you will not run away. Let go of him, Prue.'

The habit of obedience asserted itself. Mum released Dan. He stood where he was, looking at the red mark on his wrist.

'He wasn't supposed to hear,' said Hilda Selby. She attempted a smile. 'Little pitchers have big ears.'

Mum's anger hadn't cooled. It was directed as much at Grandpa as at Hilda. She faced him.

'Why did you have to tell her, anyway? You shouldn't have done. It's no concern of hers. And now the boy knows. You can't tell what harm it might do him. His whole life might be ruined, like mine!'

'Prudence,' said Grandpa, 'take your hat off and sit down.'

Mum took her hat off and sat down. Sitting, she looked more like a little girl than ever.

'I hope,' said Grandpa, 'that when you have calmed down you will tell Mrs Selby you're sorry. And perhaps you will even apologize to your own father.'

'I'm not sorry,' Mum said sullenly.

'There is something you are not yet aware of,' said Grandpa. 'Something that makes a great deal of difference. Prudence, take note. Daniel, you too may listen. Before long' – he paused impressively – 'the whole world will know. Mrs Selby – Hilda – show them what you have on your finger.'

Hilda extended a hand. Mum took a look and recoiled.

'Mrs Selby and I,' said Grandpa, 'are going to be married.'

Mum stared at him, speechless. Hilda broke the silence.

'It's for the best, Prue,' she said. 'It was for your sake we decided it, really. Yours and Dan's. I want to be a friend to you, Prue, and a second mother to your little boy.' She stretched out her arms towards Dan. 'Come to me, Dan dear,' she said.

Dan drew back. He didn't fancy Hilda's embrace, or like being called a little boy. Mum sat in tight-lipped, white-faced silence. Grandpa took the opportunity to speak.

'So you see, Prue,' he said, 'from now on, anything that is my business is Mrs Selby's business. Hilda's business.'

'I'm sorry he heard what he shouldn't, Prue dear,' said Hilda. 'I suppose I should have dropped my voice. But I'm not used to being *listened to*.'

'You have nothing to reproach yourself for, Hilda,' said Grandpa.

'You can't do it,' said Mum to Grandpa. 'Remarry. And *her*, of all people.'

'Nonsense, Prue. It is many years since your mother died. This marriage is entirely suitable. There can be no objection, in the eyes of man or of God.' He spoke confidently, as one who had no doubt of his Maker's approval.

Mum jumped to her feet. She faced them both with hatred in her eyes. 'You – you *bugger!*' she said to Grandpa; and, to Hilda, 'You *bitch!*'

Grandpa's mouth dropped open. He and Hilda stood aghast. Mum turned on her heel and rushed from the room. Room-door and street-door banged in turn behind her. Dan, bewildered, moved as if to follow.

'I think you had better stay here, Daniel,' Grandpa told him; and then, after a long pause, 'Listen carefully. I have something to say to you.' His expression was severe. 'Sometimes,' he went on, 'when we are young we hear what we ought not to have heard, or see what we ought not to have seen. Then it is our duty to put such knowledge away from us. You must forget what you have witnessed this afternoon, Dan, and in particular all that was improper and unseemly. You understand?'

He paused for Dan to make the response, 'Yes, Grandpa.'

'And you must continue to reverence your mother. It is right that a child should reverence his mother, whatever happens.'

'Yes, Grandpa.'

'You shall have your tea here,' Grandpa went on. 'It will prepare you for the coming change in this household. Mrs Selby will make tea for us both.'

'Auntie Hilda,' Hilda corrected him. 'Well, he can't call me Grandma, can he? I wouldn't venture to take his dear grandma's place. Besides,' she smiled coyly, 'I'm not really old enough to be his grandma, am I?'

'Until tea is ready,' Grandpa added, 'you may

continue reading your book.' He followed Hilda into the kitchen. It took a long time for the high tea to appear. Dan knew they were deep in conversation, because he could hear, intermittently, Hilda's penetrating voice.

Dan didn't want to listen to Hilda; he felt he had learned too much already and he didn't want to learn any more. But he didn't want to finish his book, either; the old gentleman in the story had already been a long time dying and seemed good for many pages yet.

He picked a different book at random from the shelf and began reading: more to keep Hilda's voice from his ears and to prevent himself from thinking than because he had any wish to read. But the book soon caught his attention. It was called *Stories for the Sabbath*, and the page at which he opened it was the beginning of a story about a little girl and her grandfather. The grandfather didn't look at all like Grandpa, for an elaborate line drawing showed him as magnificently bearded, whereas Grandpa was clean-shaven. Yet perhaps there was some resemblance.

The little girl, whose name was Emma, was staying at Grandfather's house. One day Grandfather placed a big, beautiful box of chocolates on the table in front of her and said, 'Emma, I am going out for a few minutes. You are not to touch the chocolates.' Off he went. Emma was tempted. She climbed on a chair, looked at the box, climbed down, walked around the room a bit, climbed back on the chair, told herself she hadn't been forbidden to lift the lid, did so, looked at the mouthwateringly delicious chocolates inside ...

It was good gripping stuff, and Dan was gripped. The temptation of Emma continued for several pages. In the end her resistance was successful. With enormous effort she refrained from touching the chocolates. Back came Grandfather. Emma ran to him, crying, 'Oh Grandfather, I was so tempted, but I have not touched the chocolates!'

Dan, misreading the message, supposed that Grandfather would be pleased. Not so. His brow darkened. He was deeply disappointed in Emma. A child with her advantages of birth and upbringing should never for a moment have been tempted. He had intended to give her the chocolates. Now she was in disgrace and would not get any.

A homily on the avoidance of temptation – it could be avoided by instant obedience to the adult will and refusal to contemplate even the possibility of any other course – concluded the story. Dan closed the book, sighing. The path of virtue was a stony one.

Hilda came in, removed the plush tablecloth and replaced it with white linen in readiness for tea. The meal, preceded and followed by a grace, consisted of slices of cold ham and tongue, with rounds of pale green tomato and a great deal of white bread. There was cake to follow. Hilda offered the plate to Dan. Three slices had been cut, and Dan had presence of mind enough to take the thinnest. It paid off. 'Isn't he a good boy?' said Hilda to Grandpa, and both looked pleased.

Afterwards Grandpa took coat, hat and scarf from the hatstand and set off with Dan for Daisy Mount. On the way he told Dan that on arrival he was to go straight to bed while Grandpa talked to Mum. Dan was warned again to forget what he had heard and not be corrupted by it – it seemed that Grandpa was as much concerned about the rude words as anything else – and was told to remember only that he was acquiring a new relative, a new influence for good.

At Daisy Mount, Mum was waiting, tense but dry-eyed.

'No, don't kiss me, Prue,' said Grandpa, though she hadn't shown any sign of doing so. 'I have serious things to say to you. And pay attention. I don't want to have to say them twice.'

Dan went straight to bed as he'd been told, and pulled the bedclothes up round his ears.

CHAPTER 4

During the next few days, the questions 'Who is my real dad? *Where* is he?' filled Dan's mind and came again and again to his lips. But he never uttered them. Mum had said she wasn't going to tell him, and Dan knew when Mum meant what she said. He held his peace.

Under his cap, the imaginary family flourished. He lived with them all the way up City Hill to the Edge School each morning, and all the way down again each afternoon. The Edge School was a small, private school run by a Mrs Sugden and her unmarried daughter, where fifty or sixty children were taught with moderate efficiency to read and write and do sums. Equally important to their parents, they were saved from going to Canal Street Elementary School, at the very foot of the hill, where they might be bullied by rough children, learn rude words, and get things in their hair.

Dan talked to his imaginary family not only on the walk to and from school but in playtime and the dinner-hour, and often in class as well. Miss Sugden called him – tolerantly or crossly, according to her mood – 'Dreamy Dan'. At present Dan was dreamier than usual. But the face of his imagined father, formerly clear in his mind's eye, had grown misty, shifting and blank. It was as if the dad of his fancy had withdrawn, waiting for someone to take his place. The real dad, whoever that might be.

Through the weekend and the earlier part of next week, Mum too was silent and subdued. Thursday was the day on which Uncle Alec often came to see her, and on which Dan always dawdled on his way home and hoped not to find the door locked against him. On the next Thursday the door was open. There was the smell of Uncle Alec's tobacco – quite different from that of Mum's occasional Woodbine – but there was no Uncle Alec. Mum, however, was bright and excited.

The excitement continued, almost feverish, on Friday. Dan was urged to get home from school promptly. Mum made him his favourite tea, of sausages and fried potatoes followed by canned peaches in syrup. After tea, she offered to play a game with him. Dan brought out the Pilgrim's Progress game, a gift from Grandpa, but Mum told him to put it away and get out the Ludo. There was a pleasant sense of wickedness about this, because playing Ludo involved the use of dice, said by some at the Chapel to be an invention of the Devil. (The Pilgrim's Progress game avoided such dubious expedients by making progress around the board dependent on the number of letters in words chosen at random from the Bible.)

At bedtime Mum gave Dan a sixpence for the next day, instead of his usual Saturday penny. She brought him a milky drink in bed, which was unusual, because she said he was over-excited and needed something to settle him. The milky drink was very sweet but had a slightly bitter taste under the sweetness. Dan had to be told firmly to drink it up. When he had done so, Mum threw her arms round him, weeping and covering his face with kisses. That was the last thing he knew that night.

Dan fell deeply asleep. He woke about noon on Saturday to find the house empty and his mother gone.

Dan went straight to Grandpa's, as Mum must have known he would do. Grandpa, baffled and increasingly worried as Mum failed to reappear, gave him meals over the weekend and made up a bed for him in the back room. On Monday a letter addressed to Grandpa arrived through the post. It was in Mum's handwriting, which Dan knew well. Grandpa took it away to read, and said nothing to Dan about the contents. On Monday night he came into Dan's room to see that Dan said his prayers, and knelt down beside him.

'Pray especially for your mother,' he said.

'Where is she?' asked Dan.

'I don't know,' said Grandpa. Grandpa was totally truthful, so this meant that he didn't know.

'Will she be coming back?'

'I don't know,' said Grandpa again.

Dan prayed as best he could, but he wasn't very good at finding things to say to God outside his usual formula. He finished, and opened his eyes. Grandpa was kneeling beside him, eyes closed and lips moving. Dan waited for what seemed a long time. Finally Grandpa turned to Dan and said, 'We must pray together.' He turned away again, closing his eyes, and began, 'Our Father, which art in Heaven . . .'

When he'd finished, he said to Dan in a steady voice, 'Let that comfort you.' But tears were running down his cheeks.

Next Saturday, Aunt Verity's husband, Uncle Bert, came round in his motorcar. This would have been an excitement for Dan, and indeed for the neighbourhood, for motorcars were still not common in the streets of City Hill. But Dan's mind was in a state of protective numbness that prevented him from feeling much interest in anything. Grandpa, Dan and Uncle Bert made three or four trips to Daisy Mount in the stuttering, oily-smelling vehicle to collect various possessions. Nothing of Dan's was left in the house.

On Sunday, after Chapel, Grandpa, Hilda and Dan

went to midday dinner at Aunt Verity's. She and Uncle Bert lived high in the Chrysanthemums close to the Edge, a grassy cleft which was City Hill's nearest approach to an open space.

After the Yorkshire pudding, roast beef and apple charlotte, Aunt Verity told Dan and her son Basil to go out and play. This was what Dan dreaded on these occasions, for he was used to being bossed and bullied by his older cousin. Today however Basil was in an unusual mood. There was greedy curiosity in his pale, lashless eyes. He took Dan into the shed at the foot of Aunt Verity's narrow garden.

'They want us out of the way,' he said. 'You know why?'

Dan said nothing.

'It's so they can talk,' said Basil. 'You know what about?'

Dan still said nothing.

'It's about your mum. You know what she's done?' Basil waited a moment but decided there wasn't going to be any response. 'She's done wrong, that's what she's done.'

Dan tried to get away, but Basil had placed himself in the doorway of the shed.

'She's been doing it for a long time,' he went on. 'A feller that came to see her without his wife knowing, every week. Grandpa didn't know and my mum didn't know. Did *you* know?'

Dan shook his head, though of course he'd known about Uncle Alec.

'They don't know much, my mum and my grandpa. They're innocent. I bet you don't know much either, do you? I bet you don't know how people do wrong.'

Dan was still silent.

'It's called . . .' Basil whispered a word, then went on, 'This is what you do,' and launched into a graphic, fairly accurate description of sexual intercourse. Then, grinning, 'I reckon your mum must like it.'

Dan was clenching his fists.

'Anyway, she's gone off now with her fancy-man,' said Basil. 'I bet they keep doing it all the time. Your mum's a tart, that's what she is.'

Suddenly Dan flew at him, bony fists whirling. Basil, though podgy, was bigger and stronger. But he was taken aback by Dan's fierce assault. Dan landed a blow in his face, which brought tears to his eyes and a bright red flow of blood from his nose. As he staggered, Dan hit him twice, hard, in the stomach. Basil turned tail and fled, wailing, into the house. Dan would have run away, but there was nowhere to go in the enclosed garden. In a minute they had both been hauled indoors to face an inquisition in Aunt Verity's parlour.

Basil was blubbering now. 'Dan hit me!' he complained between sobs.

'What? A little titch like him hit a great big feller like you?' said Uncle Bert, disgusted. 'Get away, you great softy!'

Aunt Verity's reaction was different. She rushed to the defence of her offspring. 'Dan! You *wicked* boy!' she exclaimed; and, to the others, 'I always knew there was bad blood in him!'

'What did you hit him for, Dan lad?' inquired Uncle Bert with interest.

Dan had no intention of emulating the children in Grandpa's books who wouldn't tell tales in any circumstances. He told.

'He c-c-called my mother a tart!' he said.

Grandpa, Hilda and Aunt Verity looked at each other in consternation. Basil stopped blubbering.

'I never!' he lied. 'He just hit me! He hit me for nothing!'

Grandpa stepped in to take charge. 'Basil,' he said,

'and Dan, I don't know which of you used that terrible word, but it must never again cross the lips of either of you.'

'I didn't know what it meant,' said Basil, giving himself away.

'There! It *w-w-was* him! He *did* say it!' Dan declared. But Grandpa was too shocked to apportion blame.

'You will promise me, both of you,' he said, 'by all that you hold sacred, never again to use that word.'

'I promise,' said Basil.

'By all that I hold sacred,' said Grandpa, prompting him.

'By all that I hold sacred.'

'Good. Now, Dan.'

'I-promise-by-all-I-hold-sacred,' said Dan in a rush.

Grandpa relaxed, the crisis over. 'I shall expect you both to observe your promises,' he said.

'Anyway, Prue isn't that bad,' remarked Uncle Bert. 'I can't say I blame her, married to that feller Jack Lunn. There's not been much fun in her life. She shouldn't have left the boy, though.'

The cold, condemnatory eyes of his wife, father-in-law and father-in-law's fiancée were turned upon him. Uncle Bert blushed. 'Well, time I was going,' he said, and edged towards the door.

'I think it's time these boys were on their way to Sunday School,' said Aunt Verity. 'And if you ask me, they have a great deal to learn about how they should speak and behave. Especially Dan. I'm sure he leads Basil astray.'

In view of their recent conflict, it was decided that Dan and Basil should not be sent off to Sunday School together. Aunt Verity took Basil, while Grandpa and Hilda went with Dan. Uncle Bert, risking his wife's disapproval for a breach of the Sabbath, stayed behind to spend a happy afternoon under his car.

On the way out of Sunday School, Dan and Basil had a brief encounter.

'She *is* a tart!' hissed Basil.

'She's not a tart. I'll tell!'

'If you do, *I'll* tell.'

Dan went back to Marigold Grove with Hilda. Grandpa gave him a long lecture on the need for purity in thought, word and deed, and on the superior behaviour of his Saviour while a child in the carpenter's shop. To reinforce the lesson, Dan was given only bread and butter for his tea, while Grandpa and Hilda ate pickled herrings.

In bed at night he wept, and wished he was at home with Mum. He hardly dared to wish for the unknown dad. He would even have put up with Uncle Alec.

CHAPTER 5

Mum never came back to Daisy Mount. Dan couldn't help hearing a good deal about what was going on from the remarks of the adults, especially Hilda, who reported on all developments with loud expressions of horror and indignation. It seemed that Uncle Alec had left his wife and two children in order to go off with Mum. The family had numerous relatives in the Lilies, which were quite close to the Marigolds. They were well aware of Grandpa's pious reputation, and this made them all the more inclined to blame him for Mum's misdeeds. Alec, they said, had always been a good husband and father. Mum must have led him on. Grandpa, for all his show of religion, had obviously not brought Mum up the way he should have done. It was well known that she hadn't been married any too long before Dan was born. And so on.

Hilda heard of all these reactions at the Chapel, where condemnatory remarks by anybody about anybody were fully and faithfully reported. She didn't bother to drop her voice when telling Grandpa about them. It didn't occur to Dan that Hilda, consciously or otherwise, might be very willing for such information to come to his ears; that he was a hostage given to her by her old enemy, Mum. Meanwhile, it seemed that efforts were being made in vain to trace the missing pair. They were believed to have left the city.

The wedding of Grandpa and Hilda was brought forward and took place as soon as decently possible. The ceremony was followed by an impressive tea at the Chapel rooms, with ham, tongue, chicken and salmon, and presentations were made to the happy couple on behalf of the congregation and of the Sunday School pupils. Then, with the aid of Uncle Bert and the car, Hilda moved her belongings into Marigold Grove. There was no honeymoon.

Over the next few weeks Dan realized that there was less harmony in the household than might have been expected from the union of two such virtuous people. Hilda had not owned her former house, and it turned out that her supposed private income did not exist. She had been spending the small savings of her parents and previous husband, and had remarried just in time before the money ran out.

Grandpa in turn was less well off than Hilda had supposed. He owned his home, but most of his savings had gone into the purchase of Daisy Mount, which had had to be put in Jack Lunn's name as part of the deal for Mum's marriage. Jack had heard by now of Mum's departure and had put the house up for sale. He was unlikely to give anything back to Grandpa. Anticipating a higher combined income, Grandpa had splashed most of what he still had on the wedding reception. He now had little more than the old age pension. His joint household with Hilda was not going to be a prosperous one.

On top of everything, they now had Dan to keep. Uncle Bert, who earned good wages in his job selling dog biscuits, had offered to take Dan into his own family. But Aunt Verity thought that Dan, as the offspring of a sinful woman, would be a disgrace to them and would have a corrupting influence on Basil. Since moreover neither Dan nor Basil had the least wish to live under the same roof the plan fell through and Dan remained with Hilda and Grandpa. Hilda's disillusionment grew rapidly, and her penetrating voice took on a complaining tone. She hadn't remarried in order to skimp and scrape and bring up Mum's child.

Her housekeeping quickly became parsimonious. It wasn't really her fault; she had little to spare. Dan's breakfast was, monotonously, porridge, and his tea was bread and margarine. For a while, as in the past, he got the midday dinner provided at school for a shilling a day by Mrs and Miss Sugden. But Hilda soon stopped that; it could not be afforded. Dan had to walk to Grandpa's house for dinner, which was usually an unappetizing stew.

Soon afterwards, on Hilda's insistence, Grandpa gave notice to withdraw Dan from the Edge School. The summer term was coming to an end. After the holidays he could start at Canal Street Elementary, saving the fees of two pounds a term.

Two or three times, on his way to or from school, Dan saw the thin, shabby figure of Benjy the glazier, walking on City Hill with his wooden frame, but in unconsidered obedience to Mum's instructions he dodged out of the man's way. Once Benjy came upon him from behind and startled him by asking in a soft, ingratiating voice what had happened to his mother. Dan ran away rapidly without answering, and the man, impeded by the glass he was carrying, made no attempt to pursue him.

Meanwhile the fantasy life in Dan's head became ever more intense; the imagined family were with him all the time now. Once, oblivious to the world, he began to cross the main road in front of a tram, though the driver was clanging his bell loudly enough. A passer-by rescued him and gave him a talking-to, followed by a clip over the ear for not attending. The talking-to passed straight over his head, and he was nearly killed by another tram the next day.

Dan's twelfth birthday passed unnoticed. Grandpa, pining for Mum and already regretting his remarriage, was increasingly distracted and simply forgot about it. Aunt Verity, who didn't think about Dan any more than she could help, also forgot. Hilda had never inquired about Dan's birthday. Dan didn't remind any of them. So far as they were concerned, he was a child without a birthday.

Nevertheless, he had a birthday party. It was held inside his head. All the most popular children in the school were there, and his imaginary dad organized riotously successful games at which there were prizes for everybody. Mum laid on a marvellous tea, with sausage rolls and six kinds of sandwiches and red jelly and jam tarts and lemonade and an iced cake with candles. Afterwards Uncle Bert ran some of the children home in his motorcar, with which they were all very impressed. Aunt Verity and Basil weren't there; neither were Grandpa or Hilda. Dan hadn't actually excluded them from his imaginary party; he simply hadn't thought to invite them.

After the splendid tea of his fancy, Dan sat down in Grandpa's kitchen to an actual meal of bread and

33

dripping. Grandpa and Hilda were talking to each other over his head. Tomorrow was an important, though trying, occasion for them. Mr Railton, the Minister at the Chapel, was coming to lunch. It was an unusual honour.

'He has his dinner at night,' Hilda told her husband. 'He was most insistent that we shouldn't do anything special for him. Just a light snack would be ample, he said.'

'Still, I think we should provide something palatable,' said Grandpa. 'It isn't every day we have the Minister here.'

'I knew you wouldn't want me to economize on *him*,' Hilda said with an edge to her voice, 'however much I have to economize on myself. So I went down to Dobbs's for some of their honey-roast ham.'

Dan's mouth watered at the mention of Dobbs's ham. It was famous all over City Hill: expensive but delicious, to be served with pride to special guests.

'You were quite right, Hilda,' said Grandpa. 'Dobbs's ham is not too good for a man of God.'

'I bought half a pound of it.'

Grandpa's eyebrows went up. To buy half a pound of Dobbs's ham was lavish spending indeed. But he made no comment.

Suddenly Dan was full of resentment. They'd forgotten his birthday and given him the usual plain tea, but they'd bought half a pound of Dobbs's ham for the Minister's visit. It just showed how much they cared about him. He pushed the bread and dripping away.

'Are you not hungry, Daniel?' Grandpa inquired.

'I'm not hungry for bread and dripping.'

'It's all there is!' said Hilda sharply.

Dan left it and got up from the table. Next morning he woke up hungry. His stomach yearned for food. It yearned even for the porridge which he knew would

34

have been steeping overnight. But his imagination yearned for something more than mere nourishment. His imagination yearned for the honey-roast ham that Hilda had bought. He'd had Dobbs's ham once or twice in more prosperous times, but he'd never quite appreciated the wonder of it. The firm, pink flesh, the pure, white fat, the thin outer rim of fine golden bread-crumbs that replaced the rind on Dobbs's ham . . . It was the very poetry of food. And by the time he came home from school it would have gone. He wouldn't have had so much as a taste.

Dan got up and dressed. There was no sound yet from the front bedroom. He went downstairs and through the kitchen into the pantry. The ham would be in the meat-safe.

There came into Dan's mind the story of Emma and the chocolates. He was in just the same situation. Here was he, here was the ham, and here was temptation. He hadn't actually been told not to touch the ham, but of course that went without saying. It was not for him. If he took any, it would be stealing.

He drew from the meat-safe the plate on which the ham lay in neat overlapping slices. There was just a tiny shred, no bigger than a fingernail, that was almost detached from the top slice. That could be removed, and no one would be any the wiser. And at least he would have had the *taste* of the ham. He was entitled to taste it, surely. Listening out for sounds from above, and with his heart pounding, Dan carefully removed the outlying fragment of ham and put it, gingerly, into his mouth.

And then he went mad. Suddenly he was picking up the ham with both hands and thrusting it into his mouth, slice after slice. He swallowed it half-chewed and shovel-led in more to follow. He gobbled and gulped, gobbled and gulped.

A minute later he came with equal speed to his senses,

and stared aghast at the empty plate. His throat felt as if he'd swallowed a cricket ball. He hadn't enjoyed the ham, he hadn't even tasted it. And now it was gone. His sane mind couldn't grasp the enormity of the crime. Emma in the story had been in trouble for nothing more than temptation; but he had yielded, had been possessed perhaps by the Devil. It wasn't even ordinary ham; it was special ham, almost sacred ham. It was Dobbs's ham, intended for the Minister's lunch. The punishment, divine and mortal, for a misdeed of such dimensions was beyond imagining.

Dan's hands and feet acted for him. His hands put the empty plate back in the meat-safe and fastened the door. His feet took him upstairs and back to his bedroom. His heart thudded and thumped, his face felt white, his knees were weak.

Five minutes later, the door of the front bedroom opened. Hilda's and Grandpa's voices were heard. Somebody went downstairs. The ordinary day had begun, yet the whole universe had changed. Nothing could give back the peace of mind that Dan had had a quarter of an hour ago.

Now he must go and own up. But he couldn't bring himself to do so. Sheer fright made it impossible for him to confess.

Dan went downstairs at his usual time and said nothing. Hilda gave him the usual bowl of porridge. He wasn't hungry now and could hardly swallow; the cricket ball seemed to be still stuck in his throat. He did his best to force the porridge down, but had to leave some. Hilda looked at him sourly.

'We don't waste good eatables in *this* house,' she said. 'Think of all the poor children who'd be glad of this good porridge.' She took a spoon and scraped what was left from Dan's bowl back into the pan for future use. Grandpa gave Dan a shilling so that he could have school dinner and be out of the way of Mr Railton; and he left the house five minutes earlier than usual with his crime still undiscovered.

A day of agony followed. Dan thought it even possible that Grandpa or Hilda would come to the school to take him away for punishment. Each time the schoolroom door opened, his heart bumped yet again. He gave no thought to his work, and was told off even more than usual by Miss Sugden. At dinner-time he still had no appetite and left half the meal on his plate.

Halfway through the afternoon, Mrs Sugden came in and spoke to her daughter. Miss Sugden looked gravely in Dan's direction.

'Come out here, Dan,' she said. 'Go with Mrs Sugden into the passage.'

Dan, trembling, followed the old lady from the schoolroom. Everyone was watching him. He felt as if he were on the way to the scaffold.

'Daniel,' said Mrs Sugden, 'I'm afraid something serious has happened at your grandfather's house.'

'I know,' said Dan.

'You *know*?' Mrs Sugden sounded surprised. 'Oh well, in that case perhaps it won't be quite such a shock. The message I was asked to give you is that after school you're to go straight to your Aunt Verity's house. You're not on any account to go to your grandfather's.'

CHAPTER 6

It took Dan a long time to get to Aunt Verity's house. He dawdled on the way, dreading what might happen when he arrived. Was he to be told his crime was so dreadful

37

that Grandpa could no longer tolerate his presence in Marigold Grove? Or was he being sent to Aunt Verity's in order to receive corporal punishment from Uncle Bert?

At last he stood outside his aunt's house in Chrysanthemum Avenue. It had a door-knocker in the shape of a lion's head, which stared coldly at him. Dan looked at it for some time, then gingerly raised the knocker and let it fall with so slight a tap that he didn't really expect anyone to hear.

The door opened with startling suddenness, and Basil appeared. Dan drew back automatically. But Basil's expression wasn't hostile. There was excitement in his pale eyes.

'Well, come on in, then,' he said impatiently; and, as Dan crossed the threshold, 'there's only me in the house. You heard what happened?'

Dan shook his head dumbly.

'You ain't heard? About Grandpa?'

'No.'

'He's probably dead by now!'

Dan started violently. Basil was plainly delighted by the sensation he'd caused.

'He had a heart attack. Collapsed on the kitchen floor. The doctor came and my mum's there now and Auntie Hilda isn't half in a state. It must be serious. I expect he might die any minute. That'd be funny, wouldn't it, if he died when he's only been married three months? Three months married, and dying of a heart attack!' said Basil with relish.

'B-but what brought it on?' asked Dan. He had a sudden, terrible vision of Grandpa looking at the empty plate where the ham had been and, stricken by Dan's iniquity, collapsing on the floor, never to rise again.

'I dunno. Been overdoing it, maybe?' Basil winked horribly. 'You know. *Carrying on.* Though I'd have thought he'd be too old. And who'd want to carry on with *her*?'

'Oh, shut up, can't you?' There were tears in Dan's eyes. Grandpa was his grandpa, after all. And suppose that he himself was responsible . . . ?

''Course, he might recover,' said Basil reluctantly. 'But even if he does, I expect he'll have another attack before long.'

Basil led the way into the kitchen, still trying eagerly to discuss the prospective death of Grandpa and its likely consequences. But when Dan sat unresponsive he gave up eventually.

'My mum said we was to have our tea if she didn't get back by five,' he said.

Dan still wasn't interested in food.

'Don't you want your tea, Dan?' said Basil. 'I'd have thought you'd be glad of it. You won't be getting all that much to eat at Auntie Hilda's, from what I've heard.'

Dan said nothing.

'We're having ham,' Basil told him. 'Dobbs's ham!'

Dan started again.

'What you jumping like that for? You look as if you'd seen a ghost.'

Basil went on, boastfully, 'We *often* have ham. If it isn't ham, it's tongue. Or salmon. We get red salmon, that's the dearest. You know what my dad earns? Six pounds a week, and commission. Not bad, eh?' Then, 'What you blubbering for?' Basil sensed an advantage. 'Cry, baby, cry . . .'

But Dan was past being provoked. He was in a state of mixed shock, grief and guilt. What if he'd murdered Grandpa with the aid of Dobbs's ham? And here at Aunt Verity's was Dobbs's ham, sent surely from on high to reproach him. He was torn by a great sob, just as his aunt came in. Her expression was solemn, but she wasn't weeping.

39

'Well, Mum, how is he?' asked Basil, with an expression of deep concern, though the excited gleam was still in his eye.

'Your grandpa,' said Aunt Verity, 'is as well as can be expected. It seems he's had two or three previous attacks and not said anything about them. This one's more serious. He's in bed and to be kept very quiet. But if he gets through the next day or two, there's a good chance that he'll be with us for a long time yet.' She added simply, 'We must pray that he'll be spared.'

She sat at the kitchen table, bowed her head and put her hands together. Dan joined fervently in a prayer for Grandpa. So did Basil, in loud dramatic tones. When they'd finished, Aunt Verity laid the table for tea. 'You'll be staying here for a few days,' she told Dan, 'and you must promise to behave yourself in this dark time.'

Dan promised as fervently as he'd prayed. Then they sat down to tea. But he couldn't bring himself to eat any ham.

Three days later, Dan was taken to visit Grandpa. He lay in bed, propped up on pillows, in the front bedroom at Marigold Grove. His face was white but his expression serene.

'Well, Daniel,' he said cheerfully, 'you might never again have seen me alive. But the Lord decided it should be otherwise.'

'I'm sorry you're not well, Grandpa,' said Dan.

'There is no cause for sorrow, Dan. Whether I am well or ill, whether I am spared or taken, it is His decision, and it is not for us to question it. He knows what He is doing. Always remember that, Dan. He knows what He is about.'

Dan shifted nervously on the edge of his chair.

'He has not yet seen fit to call me to Him,' Grandpa went on. 'But He may do so at any time. And I shall be ready. I have sinned, Dan, in my time. Yes, even I have sinned. But also I have repented. And though my sins be as scarlet, yet shall they be washed white as snow.'

Dan looked down at his feet. His own sin certainly was scarlet. With repentance it could be washed white. But would repentance work when you hadn't owned up and taken your punishment?

'G-grandpa,' he said, 'w-what about the ham?'

'The ham?' Grandpa looked vague. His mind was on higher things than ham.

'For the Minister's lunch the other day.'

'For Mr Railton's lunch? You think Mr Railton would be concerned with lunch, after what happened that morning? Mr Railton, Dan, is a man of God, and took no thought for his own convenience. It was a blessing that he was here, and perhaps no accident. There is a Divine providence in all things. Mr Railton went for Dr North in his motorcar, and prayed beside me in my hour of need. But *lunch*? No one, Dan, had lunch in this household on that day.'

'Th-then it wasn't missed?'

'What wasn't missed, Daniel?'

'The ham. The Dobbs's ham.'

'Daniel,' said Grandpa heavily, 'it grieves me that when I try to talk to you seriously you speak of *ham*. Remember, ham is only flesh, and all flesh is as grass. I want you to consider, Dan, that it is quite possible you will not look upon my face again. Tomorrow, or the day after, or perhaps even in an hour's time, perhaps in the next minute, in the very middle of a sentence, I may be called away from you.'

Dan felt at once a huge lightening of the heart and the onset of tears. A lightening of the heart, because it was plain that the shock of the stolen ham was not responsible for Grandpa's illness, and an onset of tears at the thought of Grandpa's death.

'And when my Maker calls me,' Grandpa continued, 'I shall go. I shall go with a lightsome heart. I shall die happy. I pray that my last words may be "Thy will be done."'

Grandpa smiled with almost unearthly radiance. Sitting propped up in bed, his face white against the white pillow, he seemed more saintly than ever. Tears rolled down Dan's cheeks. Grandpa observed them with approval.

'Well may you weep,' he said. 'Though a child weeps for that which it does not understand, yet its grief is no less true. But, Dan, when I am gone, remember my words and think upon them. And remember the Fifth Commandment, "Honour thy father and thy mother." I hope it will not be long before your mother comes back. If she knew what had happened, she would be here at once, there is no doubt. Until she returns you must honour your Aunt Verity and your Aunt Hilda in her place, and you must obey them also, for obedience is pleasing in the sight of God.'

'And . . . my dad?' whispered Dan. 'How can I . . .?'

'What, Daniel? Speak up.'

'H-how can I honour my dad when I don't know who he is?'

Grandpa was untroubled by this question.

'If your earthly father is not at hand,' he said, 'then you must honour your heavenly Father all the more. And all else shall be added unto you. You understand?'

Dan nodded uncertainly.

'Good,' said Grandpa. 'I am content.'

There was a sound of heavy footsteps from the stairs. The door opened and Uncle Bert came in with a tray, which he plonked down on the bed.

'Hello there, Dad,' he said cheerfully. 'How are you today? Looking a bit better, I reckon.'

'Perhaps so,' said Grandpa doubtfully, as if he

thought improvement might be lacking in reverence. 'I'm still feeling a little pain now and then. A reminder, as it might be . . .'

'Don't worry about that!' said Bert. 'I'd be thankful for a bit of pain if I was you. There's plenty in the graveyard that'd be glad of a twinge or two. Look, I brought you a nice bowl of Verity's home-made soup. Sup it up, it'll put some colour in your cheeks!'

Grandpa looked at Bert with resigned patience. It was obviously no use expecting seemly attitudes from Bert.

'If the Lord meant me to eat,' he observed severely, 'He would make me feel like eating.'

Bert pulled a face and turned to Dan.

'As for you, young man,' he said, 'it looks to me as though you been crying. Come on now, that won't do. Stop worrying. Your grandpa's going to live to be a hundred, aren't you, Dad?'

'I shall live for as long as my Maker wishes and no longer,' said Grandpa with dignity; and, to Dan, 'Good-bye, Daniel. We may never meet again in this world. In that case you must rejoice that I have gone to a better one.'

But it seemed that the interview with Dan had stimulated Grandpa's appetite after all. He picked up a spoon and, pausing only for a swift grace, began eating soup with no further sign of reluctance.

'There's some soup for you, too, downstairs,' Uncle Bert said to Dan. 'Off you go, now. Enjoy it. Leave me to cheer your grandpa up.'

Dan set off down the stairs. Halfway down, he paused. He could hear the voice of Hilda, in conversation with Aunt Verity. Aunt Verity's remarks came in a barely audible mumble, but Hilda's voice as always was loud and clear. And instantly it was plain to Dan that he hadn't got away with the theft of the ham.

43

'Every scrap gone!' Hilda was saying. 'Every single bit! Well, it must have been him, mustn't it? Mind you, I haven't said a word to Percy. It would kill him. He thinks the world of that boy, I don't know why. Just wait till I get the lad on his own!'

Mumble, mumble, mumble, came the voice of Aunt Verity.

'And I'll tell you this,' Hilda went on. 'I never bargained for taking on a *boy*. Not at my age. And *such* a boy! So quiet, you never know what he's thinking, but it surely isn't anything good. I've always thought he was sly. And now we know he's a *thief*!'

Mumble, mumble, mumble, from Aunt Verity. Dan stood still on the stairs, listening hard.

'Well, if anything happens to Percy – and Dr North says I must be prepared for it – I won't be responsible for the boy, and that's flat. If Prue doesn't come and take him, I reckon the best place for him is Broad Street children's home!'

Mumble, mumble, mumble, with a note of surprise.

'Well, I will say this for you, Verity, you're not one to shirk your duty. But would it be fair to your own, if you were to have him? I know what you think about him being a bad influence on your Basil . . . Wait a minute! Where is he now?'

The kitchen door was flung open. A moment later, Hilda stood at the foot of the stairs, looking up at Dan.

'What are you doing there?' she demanded. Her voice seemed to vibrate right through him as he shrank to the side of the staircase. 'Have you been *listening*?'

For the second time in a week, Dan's body acted without any reference to his mind. He found himself charging headlong down the stairs, butting Hilda in the midriff, ducking beneath her outstretched arm, and racing from the house into the street.

Three thoughts – three huge, brutal thoughts – bat-

44

tered his brain as he sped away through the Marigolds.

Grandpa was dying. Nobody wanted him. He would be homeless.

CHAPTER 7

Dan's feet took him automatically where they'd have taken him at any time for years past: to Mum's house in Daisy Mount. That was where he'd lived all his life. But now everything was changed. An estate agent's board was fixed to the front of the house, and over the words FOR SALE had been stuck at an angle a strip saying SOLD.

The curtains were still in the front windows, but there was nothing behind them. Dan went round to the back. He needed a refuge – any refuge – where he could be on his own for a while and think things over. There was just a chance that a key to the house might remain, forgotten, in the usual hiding-place.

The key wasn't there, but the back door, surprisingly, was unlocked. Dan went into the living-room. There was an old sofa still there that Grandpa and Uncle Bert hadn't thought worth taking away. And sprawling on it, fast asleep with his head resting on a rolled-up jacket, was Jack Lunn. The air around him was thick with the smell of drink.

Dan stood looking at him for a minute. He wasn't afraid of Jack, who had never laid a finger on him, but he was afraid of the drink. Grandpa was a crusading teetotaller, and many of his storybooks featured the Demon Drink, whose victims died of starvation in the gutter.

Not that Jack Lunn looked or sounded as if he was dying. He was a big, heavy-bellied man, full of blood. His bullet head was cropped almost like a convict's, and there was two or three days' ginger stubble on his broad, flushed cheeks. He was snoring loudly.

Dan backed away, his eyes still on Jack's face, then stumbled heavily over something on the floor, and fell. The snoring stopped. Dan got up to see Jack's open, bloodshot eyes watching him from the makeshift pillow. Painfully Jack raised his head, slewed his body round and put his feet to the ground. Then he said, 'It's Danny. How do, Danny. Long time since I saw you. What time is it?'

Dan didn't have a watch, but as if in answer to Jack's question the clock on St Jude's Church down the road struck the hour. One o'clock.

'Blimey. I been asleep all morning.' Jack put his hands to his head, shook it, and winced. 'Musta had a skinful last night. Here, hold on a minute. Don't run away. You're not scared of your dad, are you?'

The words pulled Dan up short. 'You're not my dad,' he said.

'Oh?' said Jack. He rubbed his bloodshot eyes. 'Pass me them fags, Danny.'

Dan passed him the open cigarette packet which lay on the floor.

'You're not, are you?' he insisted. 'You're not my dad?'

Jack Lunn lit up. 'We-e-ell,' he said in a casual tone, as if it didn't matter very much, 'maybe so, maybe not. Somebody's said summat to you about it, eh, lad?'

'Yes. My mum and my grandpa and my new auntie, they all say you aren't.'

'Aye, well, if that's what they say, I won't argue with it. I promised I'd never tell, but if the cat's out of the bag, all right then, fair enough. It's true, Danny. You was

46

well on the way before I had anything to do with your mum.'

'Then who's my real dad?'

'Nay, that I don't know. Wasn't none of my business, was it? I knew you was coming, and your grandpa wanted your mum wed. Well, I quite fancied her; she was a bonny 'un, your mum, and still is. And with a rent-free house thrown in, I reckoned it was a good deal. I didn't ask no questions; I wasn't supposed to.'

'But I want to know,' said Dan.

Jack drew on his cigarette and considered the matter. 'Aye,' he conceded, 'I can see that you might.'

'How am I going to find out?'

'Nay, I don't know, Danny. It was a long time ago. I reckon nobody knows except your grandpa and your mum and the chap in question, and if they've kept it dark all these years they'll not be telling you now.'

'But I *need* him. I don't like it with Hilda or Aunt Verity, and they don't like me. And I don't want to go into a home!'

'There, there, lad,' said Jack. 'Don't get into a state. If I was a different sort of feller, I'd try and be a dad to you myself. But you can see, can't you, it's not my line.' He added, in the tone of one giving a friendly word of warning, 'I wouldn't rely on *me*, if I was you.' And then, as if suddenly struck by an interesting recollection, 'I must say, I used to have my suspicions, years ago, about who it might have been.'

'Who?' asked Dan eagerly.

'Listen, Danny, you got a middle name, haven't you?'

'Yes,' said Dan. 'Hunter. Nobody uses it, though.'

'You ever thought where that name comes from?'

'I think my mum said it was the name of some relatives. I don't know, I never met them.'

'She told me that, too, and *I* never met them, neither.

47

Now, Danny, you ever heard of Hunter Engineering?'

''Course I've heard of Hunter Engineering,' said Dan. Hunter Engineering was one of the biggest employers in the city.

'Well, Danny, the proper name of that firm is Daniel Hunter and Sons Limited. The Hunter family's been around in this city for donkeys' years, and there's been two or three Daniels that I know of. It's a family name. Now, the present Hunters live in a big house at High-wood, on top of the hill, a mile or two from here. Suppose, young Danny, just suppose . . .'

A knowing look came to Jack Lunn's face.

'Suppose some young scallywag in *that* family had been paying court to your mum. And suppose you was the result. They wouldn't have let him marry her, would they? They'd want him to marry a Lady Somebody, or at any rate someone rich. Most likely, he wouldn't have admitted what he'd been up to. And your mum wasn't one to make scenes. She was shy, like, and only a lass herself. But just think, Danny . . .'

Jack was carried away by the force of his own fancy.

'You might have a *rich* dad if you did but know it,' he said. 'A dad with money and houses and motorcars and a big company and I don't know what!'

Dan said nothing. His mind had just been blown apart. He had imagined a dad with a steady job and good wages, but never anything more spectacular than that. Now, suddenly, he was faced with the idea of wealth and grandeur, and it was more than he could cope with. He stood in wide-eyed silence.

Jack Lunn realized the effect his words were having, and backpedalled hastily. 'Mind you,' he said, 'it's only a thought. I don't know that I'd take it too seriously. In fact, Danny, if I was you I wouldn't take it seriously at all.'

Jack would have withdrawn the suggestion if he could.

But it was too late. The words had been said. It would take more than Jack's second thoughts to remove the notion from Dan's head. He might be a rich man's son. Such things happened frequently in Grandpa's storybooks. Poor, shabby children of noble character turned out to be the offspring of secret marriages long ago between people of high social standing; quite often indeed they were heirs to titles. The Hunter connection seemed very probable.

'It was just a daft idea I used to have,' said Jack. 'I oughtn't to 'a' mentioned it.'

'B-but it *could* be true, couldn't it?'

'It *could*,' said Jack, still backpedalling, 'but you can bet your boots it ain't. Go back to your Grandpa's, Danny, and don't think no more about it.'

'I'm not at Grandpa's. I'm at Aunt Verity's. Grandpa's ill. He's had a heart attack.'

'Eh, I didn't know that!' Jack Lunn was shocked. He asked two or three questions, which Dan answered as best he could. 'Poor old Pious Percy! He could be trying sometimes, but I always had a soft spot for him. Thought he could reform the world, your Grandpa did. He even thought he could reform *me*!'

Jack chuckled reminiscently.

'He knew I was sleeping rough, but he reckoned if I married his daughter and had a house of my own I'd be a changed character. He never realized that human nature don't work like that. A settled life ain't my way, Danny. I get uneasy if I sleep in the same place too many nights running. I hadn't been married a month before I was slipping away, two or three nights a week maybe, to a hideout I had, down on the canal bank. It wasn't that I was tired of your mum or anything like that, it was just that I felt fenced in. I needed my freedom, Danny. A good place that was, where I used to go. It's still there, still a good place, nobody knows about it.'

'Where is it?' Dan asked.

Jack, who'd been reminiscing mainly to keep the conversation away from Dan's supposed Hunter connection, was quite willing to go on talking.

'It's down along Canal Street,' he said, 'right by the railway viaduct. I was there a few days ago. There's a row of derelict cottages, and over the top of them all there's an attic. Bone dry and comfortable, you'd never guess from outside. Go round the gable end, almost under the arch, shin up the drainpipe, put your foot where there's a brick missing, and in you go through the window. No trouble at all. There's a mattress in there and a paraffin stove, and there's a standpipe in the yard behind for water. What more do you need? Rent, nothing per week. Now that I've sold this house I'd go back there myself if I wasn't leaving the city.'

'Why are you leaving the city?' Dan asked.

'There's one or two spots of bother I'm in. Nothing serious, but I'll be better going away for a while.'

'I'm in trouble, too,' said Dan.

'*You*? You in trouble, Danny? I don't believe it. You're not the type. What you been up to?'

'I ate the ham for the Minister's lunch.'

'You ate *what*?' A grin spread slowly over Jack Lunn's face. His shoulders heaved. Finally he roared with laughter. 'You ate the Minister's dinner? That's rich, that is. I wish I coulda seen their faces!'

'Nobody else thinks it's funny,' said Dan.

'Why did you do it, lad? Was you hungry?'

'Yes,' said Dan. 'But I didn't mean to eat it *all*. It just sort of happened.'

'Haven't they been feeding you?'

'I didn't do very well at Grandpa's,' Dan admitted. 'I've been at Aunt Verity's since he was ill. *She* feeds me all right. But I don't feel welcome there. And she's only just heard about the ham. She'll want me even less after that, and Auntie Hilda won't have me at all. I'll probably be put in Broad Street.'

'Now listen, lad,' said Jack. At last he was fully serious. 'I know your Aunt Verity. She may complain, but she'd never put you in an orphanage. You go and make your peace with her, that's my advice.'

Dan pulled a face at the prospect.

'You've had a rough time lately, haven't you, lad?' said Jack with some sympathy. 'Whereas I'm coming out of it all right, I must admit. I'm getting four hundred quid for this house. Not bad, eh? I've borrowed forty on the strength of it already.'

Dan said nothing. Sums of this size were beyond his comprehension.

'Mind you, I've always tret your mum fairly. I wouldn't have thrown her out, even now. She threw herself out, didn't she? You can't blame me for cashing in.' Jack paused for thought. 'All the same . . .' he added, and paused again. He rummaged in a jacket pocket, drew out a handful of crumpled notes, and thrust most of them at Dan. 'Here you are, lad. I reckon you've a right to some of it.'

Dan stared at him, still bemused.

'Go on, Danny, take it!' said Jack. 'It's yours. Keep it from all them relatives if you can. It might come in handy some day. It's no good *me* keeping it. I'd only spend it in the pubs, if I didn't lose it on horses. In fact, when I get the rest of the money I dare say I'll be drunk for a year.' He shook his head as if in sorrow at his own improvidence, then winced once more.

'I could do with summat to eat,' he said. 'And what about you, Danny? Are you hungry now? Listen, there's a chippy just a few yards down the main road. Why don't I go and get us some fish and chips?'

'I'll come with you,' Dan offered.

'No, you stay here. I might just nip into the George for

a quick pint on the way, and you can't go in, being under age. I'll bring the grub and we'll eat it here, for old times' sake. I won't be long. See you soon, Danny.'

No doubt Jack Lunn meant to do just as he'd said. But he didn't carry out his intention. Dan never saw him again.

CHAPTER 8

Left alone, Dan wandered round the house. It didn't feel like home any more. Only two or three items of useless broken-down furniture and a few strips of worn linoleum remained. The sound of his boots echoed from bare floorboards and uncarpeted stairs. His own bedroom at the back, now totally empty, seemed surprisingly small and stripped of all its memories.

In Mum's room at the front, a double brass bedstead still stood. It brought to his mind the unwelcome thought of Uncle Alec. He went out of the room quickly and down to the front parlour. Here again were bare boards; and on a window-ledge, lying face down, was a postcard-sized photograph frame. Dan picked it up. The picture was of Mum, delicately posed on a sofa in what looked like a beautiful drawing-room but was in fact the studio of Bright's, the photographers on City Hill. Mr Bright's flowing signature ran across the foot of the sepia print.

It must have been taken a few years before. Mum looked very young, very pretty and very happy. Dan felt a moment's pride in being the son of this lovely young woman. The photograph, complete with frame, would just go into his pocket. He slid it in, and went back to the living-room, where the smell of drink still lingered. He lay on the old sofa where Jack had been and, inspired by the photograph, tried to conjure up a new version of the old daydream. Dad was rich and handsome, Mum was more beautiful than ever, and they were surrounded by luxury . . . But he hadn't much idea of what it would be like to be rich and surrounded by luxury, and such imagining was hard work. In two or three minutes he was asleep.

The sound of St Jude's Church clock striking the hour woke him. Three o'clock. He'd been here two hours. There was no sign of Jack or of the fish and chips. The George would be closed by now, and so would the chip shop. There was no telling what Jack had got up to. He might come back and he might not. If he did come back, he might be sober and he might not. In any case he wouldn't stay long; he never did. It was no good relying on Jack for anything.

Dan put his feet to the ground and stood up. He felt strangely clear-headed, as if he'd been living in a mist which had lifted. With a flash of what seemed to him like uncanny brilliance, he knew what his next move would be. He wouldn't go back, either to Aunt Verity's or to Hilda's. He would survive on his own. He would find his real dad and reunite him with Mum. With the clue Jack had given him, he was sure he could manage it. But it might take a little time. Where would he live while he carried out his quest?

Once more the answer flashed into his mind. He would set himself up in the place Jack Lunn had told him of, down at the end of Canal Street, by the railway viaduct. After all, he now had money. He pulled the notes from his pocket and counted them. Twelve pounds. He'd never seen so much money in his life. He could live for months on twelve pounds. Surely he wouldn't need *that* long.

But he'd need to do something to prevent a search being mounted for him. The third flash of brilliance came to him. He would leave a note at Aunt Verity's that would deter any pursuit.

He had a stub of pencil in his pocket. On the floor inside the front door, lying unregarded, were three or four letters, bills and circulars. He tore them open until he found a circular with a blank reverse side. On it he wrote:

MY MUM CAME. SHE HAS TAKEN ME
AWAY. LOVE FROM DAN.

He put the circular, refolded with his own message on the outside, back in its envelope and wrote AUNT VERITY on the front. At this point, conscience taxed him with the lie. Grandpa, and Grandpa's books, had made it clear that even the tiniest of lies was a grave sin. This was a big lie. To be on the safe side, Dan crossed his fingers and promised to repent later. Having thus appeased his conscience, he felt free to congratulate himself on his scheme. It would surely satisfy Hilda and Aunt Verity. They wouldn't question the message. 'Prue must have taken him after all,' they'd say. 'Good riddance.' Well, good riddance to them, too.

Dan put the readdressed letter in his pocket, along with the pound notes. From the other pocket he drew the picture of Mum and studied it afresh. She looked out at him from a different world, innocent and charming. But she was the same person, whatever she'd done since then. Dan felt a surge of loyalty. He resolved to carry the picture with him from now on, wherever he went. He put it back in his pocket, feeling its comfortable angularity. Then he set out boldly for Aunt Verity's.

Dan felt more confidence in himself than he'd ever felt before, but he didn't let this make him rash. He chose a careful route through the side-streets, steering well clear of Grandpa's house, and he edged his way cautiously into Chrysanthemum Avenue. The last thing he wanted now was an encounter with his aunt and Uncle Bert. But there was no sign of life from the house with the lion-knocker door, and Uncle Bert's car was not parked in its usual place outside.

That was good. They must be still at Grandpa's. Dan had intended merely to put his message through Aunt Verity's letter-box and make himself scarce. Now a new thought came to him: why not pick up some of his belongings? He couldn't wear the clothes he was standing up in indefinitely, and if he had to buy new clothing it would make a hole in his capital.

Aunt Verity was always careful to lock her back door, but Dan knew how to get in through the little window of the outside lavatory. It only took him seconds. He crept up the back stairs to his room, a second-floor attic, in which his possessions were tidily arranged in accordance with instructions from Aunt Verity. He stuffed what he could into the battered leather satchel which he normally carried to school, then left his note prominently displayed on the dresser and hurried down the stairs. And just as he reached the first landing the bathroom door opened. Basil came out and stood in his way.

For a moment Basil seemed as startled as Dan was. Then his eye fell on the bulging satchel, which Dan was trying vainly to hide behind himself. 'Hey, what you got there?' he demanded.

'Only my own things.'

'Where you going with them?' Basil asked. But he didn't wait for an answer. He went on triumphantly, 'Don't you know they're looking for you? My mum said if you came back you was to stay here till she and my dad got home. I'm going to keep you here! You'll be for it! I expect my dad'll belt you!'

Dan said nothing. He was assessing his chances of getting past Basil and out of the house.

'And Grandpa so poorly, too!' added Basil sanctimoniously.

'Is he worse?' Dan asked.

'Not that I know of. Not since this morning, anyway. But he's as pale . . . as pale as *death*, my mum says. He'll be took away in a box before long!'

'He mightn't,' said Dan. 'He might get better.' He slid the satchel from his shoulder, and his fingers tightened round the strap of it.

'He'll die all right,' said Basil confidently. 'It was a bad attack and he's had others. The doctor told my mum . . .'

His mind full of the interesting prospect of Grandpa's demise, Basil was off guard. Dan swung the satchel and socked him hard in the midriff. Basil staggered back gasping, bumped into the bathroom door, slipped, and ended up sitting on the floor. Dan sped past him, leaped down the stairs two at a time, and was out through the front door, slamming it behind him. Within a minute he'd disappeared round two or three corners. After another minute he slowed to a walking pace. Podgy, sluggish Basil, even if he'd recovered his breath, didn't have a hope of catching him, and probably wouldn't try.

By devious routes, through the Chrysanthemums and Marigolds and Daisies, downhill all the way from the respectable upper streets through the humbler Primroses and Violets to the sooty disreputable depths of the Jungle, Dan made his way. He was heading for Canal Street and the row of derelict cottages beside the railway viaduct.

CHAPTER 9

Nobody knew why the Jungle was so called. It may have been something to do with the fancy street names: Orchid, Camellia, Mimosa, Hibiscus and others, so much more florid than the homely Marigolds and Daisies farther up the hill. These exotic names were in stark contrast to the reality, for it was a place of crumbling black brickwork, of small shabby shops and workplaces, and row upon row of squat terraced houses stretching down to the North West Junction Canal. Yet the Jungle was well named: it was a tangle in which any stranger could rapidly get lost, and in which fierce creatures were said to prowl.

Children in particular, if their homes were outside the Jungle, took care not to stray into it. Gangs of lads roamed its streets: lean, ragged lads who, it was said, would have murdered their grannies for a shilling. That was an exaggeration, of course. Yet Dan should have known he ought to be careful. He had a fortune of twelve pounds in his pocket; he was carrying a satchel, and although he wasn't wearing the Edge School cap, which would have been asking for trouble, his jacket had a school badge sewn on to a top pocket. He was a natural prey for the Jungle denizens.

Normally he'd have gone down to the canal by way of the main thoroughfares, Camellia Hill and Hibiscus Street. Near the bottom of Hibiscus Street stood the police station, which cast a protective aura of law and order for some distance around. He'd have been quite safe if he'd taken that route. But Dan's confidence had increased to a dangerous degree. He decided to cut off a corner by threading his way through a web of narrow streets, intending to come out by the side of the elementary school, halfway along Canal Street.

There weren't many people around in the little streets: a few housewives chatting in doorways, small dirty children playing in the gutters, two or three old jossers hobbling along. It was still broad daylight: somewhere around teatime. All the same, before he'd gone far Dan began to feel a little uneasy and to have a sense of being watched by unseen eyes. He moved warily, regretting his rashness and ready to take to his heels at any sign of trouble. But nothing happened, and by the time he reached the back wall of the school his confidence was coming back. At the other side of the school was Canal Street, open and safe. He reckoned that any danger there might have been was now past.

He was wrong. They'd seen him coming. They'd followed him all the way from Hibiscus Street, waiting to get him in a quiet place. As he passed the school railings, with safety only a few yards away, they leaped out from behind the cover of a high wall, and before he could even shout they'd dragged him into a nearby alleyway. They surrounded him: two lads of about his own age and two a little older. They were pale and poorly dressed and none of them had any kind of weapon, but there was a scrawny toughness about them that came from years of surviving in the Jungle.

The two younger ones grabbed Dan's arms. A third boy, with a round, goblinesque face, twisted the satchel out of his grip.

'What's in it, Charlie?' said the fourth boy, who seemed to be the leader. Dan liked the look of him least of all. He was tall, skinny, narrow-eyed and sour-faced.

Charlie opened the satchel and looked with disgust at the contents, which were principally Dan's shirts and underclothes. He tipped them to the ground and dropped the bag on top of them.

'Where you from, kid?' asked Narrow-Eyes.

As always when he was under pressure, Dan was overcome by his stammer. He couldn't get any answer to come out.

'D-d-d-d–' he began, intending to say 'Daisy Mount.' His captors were delighted. 'D-d-d-d,' they chanted. 'D-d-d-d. D-d-d-d.' Dan closed his mouth and left them to it, but after half a minute Narrow-Eyes said, 'Well, then d-d-d– what?'

'The Daisies,' said Dan, getting some words out at last.

'Oh, the Daisies.' By Jungle standards the Daisies were posh, a long way up the hill. 'What you doing down here, then?'

'J-j-j-just going for a w-w-w-w–' Dan was struggling again. He intended to say that he was going for a walk.

'W-w-w-w,' chanted the two younger boys.

'Going for a wee-wee,' said Charlie, who seemed to be the wit of the group. He continued, in tones of exaggerated maternal refinement, 'You want a wee-wee, lovey?'

The other three laughed. 'You can have a pee here if you want,' said one of the younger boys, who had sores on his face and decayed front teeth. 'Nobody's watching, 'cept us.'

Narrow-Eyes seized on the suggestion.

'Yeah, why not? Come on, what you waitin' for? Do it here!'

All four stood around him. Dan's alarm rose towards panic. He didn't know what unspeakable ordeal he might be facing.

'I d-d-don't want that,' he told them. 'I was saying, I'm going for a w-w-w-w–' – he forced the word out – 'a *walk*!'

'Go on, you want to pee,' said Narrow-Eyes. 'Get on with it. Let's be seeing you. Do it against this wall!'

'Or do you need help?' inquired Charlie. 'Shall we get your thing out for you?'

There were sniggers from the other three. Then the boy with bad teeth created a diversion.

'He's got summat in his pocket!' he said.

It was the angular shape of the photograph frame that had drawn his attention. He dipped into Dan's pocket and pulled it out. The others gathered round.

'*She's* a bit of all right,' said Narrow-Eyes.

At this point they all became aware that an older, bigger and much burlier lad was standing nearby, watching the proceedings with some amusement. He had villainously cropped red hair and a strawberry birthmark on one cheek. He looked sixteen or seventeen.

'It's Leo,' said Narrow-Eyes; and then, with some respect, ''lo, Leo. How's it going?'

Leo came over to the group.

'Let's have a look,' he said to Narrow-Eyes. He stretched out a hand for the picture and studied it with interest.

'Who is it?' he asked Dan.

Dan said nothing.

'Is it your sister?'

'N-no.'

'Who is it, then?'

'It's my m-m-mum,' Dan said reluctantly.

'M-m-m-mum!' chanted the two younger lads. 'Who's his mummy's boy, then?' asked Charlie.

'Shut up, will you?' said Leo impatiently; then, to Dan, 'She looks young. Is she really your mum?'

Dan nodded. Leo studied the picture for another half-minute. Then he said, 'I like her. I'm having this.' And he slid it into his own pocket.

'Y-y-you c-c-can't!' Dan declared indignantly. 'It's mine!'

Leo looked at him quizzically.

'Give it me!' Dan demanded, the stammer disappearing.

'Hark at *him*!' said Charlie.

'You going to take it from me?' Leo inquired. 'What's your name? Did I hear it right? Daisy?'

The four who made up the original group sniggered.

'Daisy, Daisy, give us your answer, do!' sang Charlie.

'Let go his arms, lads,' Leo said. 'Give him a chance. He's going to take his photo back.'

Dan was released.

'Well, Daisy, what about it?' Leo said. 'You going to hit me?' His own arms were at his sides, and he pushed his chin forward invitingly. 'Go on, Daisy, hit me!'

It was madness on Dan's part, but before he knew what he was doing he had hit Leo hard on the cheek with a bare clenched fist. Narrow-Eyes jumped in to attack him, and Dan hit Narrow-Eyes in turn: a hard blow on the breast-bone. Narrow-Eyes, recovering, advanced on him menacingly.

'Hold it, Doug!' said Leo. Narrow-Eyes held off and looked expectantly at Leo. Dan closed his eyes, awaiting retribution.

Leo rubbed his cheek, where a red patch was already evident. He looked down at Dan thoughtfully from a six-inch advantage in height. 'Do you know what I could do to you, Daisy?' he asked.

Dan was silent.

'I could tear you into little bits and scatter them in the street,' said Leo. He made motions with his hands as if doing so, and put on an expression of extreme ferocity. Dan shuddered.

'He's wetting hisself *now*!' said Narrow-eyes with satisfaction. 'Go on, Leo, belt him!'

Suddenly Leo grinned. He took the photograph from his pocket and handed it back to Dan. 'I wouldn't carry that around if I was you,' he said.

The other lads stared.

'You mean – you mean you ain't hitting him?' said Narrow-Eyes faintly.

'Not just now. I don't feel like it. Nor are you, Doug. Put his stuff in his bag and give it back to him.'

Narrow-Eyes was clearly outraged. For a moment it looked as if he might rebel. But Leo was in control of the situation. Helped by the boy with bad teeth, Narrow-Eyes reluctantly picked up Dan's belongings, shoved them into the satchel and handed it back to him.

'What's your real name, Daisy?' asked Leo.

'D-d-d-dan.'

This time, nobody imitated the stammer.

'Bugger off, Dan,' said Leo, 'before I change my mind. And watch your step in future. You won't always get away with it like this. Go on, off you go!'

Dan could hardly believe in his freedom. He turned away, half expecting a fresh assault. He wouldn't have been surprised if Leo had been playing cat and mouse with him. But no one followed or said anything more. The only sounds were those of his boots on the stone setts and, a moment later, the mournful muffled hoot of a ship's siren from the Sea Canal, half a mile away. And then he was safe in Canal Street. He had his satchel, his clothes and the photograph, and they'd never found his money.

Dan was buoyed up by a sense of his own worth. He'd stood up to Leo, and Leo had respected him for it. He held his head high as he strode along towards the railway viaduct and the row of abandoned cottages.

CHAPTER 10

Dan had no fears in Canal Street. It ran through bare open spaces and offered no cover for prowlers. Jungle dwellers stayed in their own closely spun web of streets and left it to its emptiness.

Once it had led to the main basin of the North West Junction Canal. Along it had been warehouses and yards and other canal company property. Then the railway had come along and the viaduct over the canal had been built. It had cut off this end of the street from the main basin. And within a few years the railway had driven the canal company out of business. Now Canal Street was a dead street. Nearly all the buildings along it had been pulled down.

It took Dan just five minutes to get to the viaduct. The row of cottages was at this side of it, right down on the canal bank. The cottages had been there before the railway and had probably been occupied by canal company employees. But nobody occupied them now. Nobody even bothered to pull them down. They'd simply been abandoned.

The four cottages had not a door or window between them. Dan's heart sank as he looked inside each one in turn. There was a great deal of rubbish, and on one of the earth floors were the remains of a bonfire where somebody, some time, had camped. There were unpleasant smells of damp and cats.

But Dan remembered what Jack Lunn had said, and walked round the outside of the little row. The gable end faced on to the supports of the railway viaduct, a mere three or four feet away. It was as if the viaduct had been flung across the canal and had just managed to miss the cottages. This was a dark, isolated corner and not over-looked: not even from the railway, as the angle was too steep.

Dan wouldn't have thought to look upward if it hadn't been for what Jack had told him. But he did; and high in the gable end he saw a door. It was an ordinary, paint-less, closed wooden door, and rather odd-looking because there was nothing in front of it but a twenty-foot drop to the ground. Beside it was a grime-encrusted window, and not far from that, at the corner of the building, was a bracket which must formerly have held an outside lamp.

The drainpipe was still there, and if big heavy Jack could climb it, then a small light person like himself could do so. He swung the satchel round to his back. Then he gripped the pipe and swarmed up it, using hands and feet alternately, slipping back once or twice and getting grime on his clothes.

In a minute, to his own surprise, Dan was on a level with the window. If he'd stopped to think what he was doing he'd have been frightened; so he didn't stop to think. He stretched out a hand to the lamp bracket, which felt firm enough, then put the toe of his boot into a tiny gap in the brickwork. Transferring the other hand to the bracket and maintaining his toehold as he shifted his weight, he was able to reach the window frame. It was an old sash window and it slid up easily. In seconds he was wriggling through, and in a few more seconds he stood safely inside.

He was in an attic which ran over the tops of all four cottages. Along the middle of it, under the ridge of the roof, it was high enough for a grown person to stand upright, but the sides sloped steeply down. It had three windows, all thick with dirt. Such light as there was came from the window Dan had just opened, and even that one was overshadowed by the viaduct. It smelled much drier up here than down below, however, and the boarded floor seemed sound.

As Dan's eyes grew accustomed to the poor light, he saw that there was a mattress on the floor, with two or three rough grey blankets. The attic also contained a broken-down armchair, a battered chest of drawers, an orange-box divided across the middle to make shelving, and a couple of rugs. There was a paraffin stove with a can of fuel beside it, and on the chest were a candle in a saucer and a box of matches. Dust lay thick on everything.

The place had been lived in: by Jack Lunn from time to time, he knew, and probably by others. Clearly it was *possible* to live here. Equally clearly, from the undisturbed dust, nobody had been here recently.

Dan felt a moment's alarm when he heard a loud, prolonged rumble, sounding as close as if it were in the next room and making the whole building vibrate. But it was only a train crossing the viaduct. A minute later he heard St Jude's Church clock, its chimes floating clearly down the hill. He counted the strokes. Six o'clock. It dawned on him that he was hungry: achingly hungry. He'd had nothing to eat since breakfast at Aunt Verity's, ten hours before.

Well, he had money: a great deal of it. And the chip shops would be open again by now. There was a small, scruffy one right down at the bottom of Hibiscus Street, not very far from here. He could have not only chips but fish. His mouth watered at the thought of piping-hot flaky white fish in crisp batter: a rare feast. And after he'd eaten he could buy food to bring home with him. Hibiscus Street was full of little shops of the kind that stayed open until all hours.

He scraped peepholes in the dirt that encrusted the

windows, to make sure there was no one about when he set out from his attic. And all was well. Canal Street was as empty as ever. Hunger gave Dan courage for his first descent by way of bracket, toehold and drainpipe; and it wasn't really too difficult. He knew he'd soon get used to it.

He could smell the chip shop long before he got to Hibiscus Street. Connoisseurs of fish and chips didn't rate this particular shop very highly; it was none too clean and its fat was said to be sometimes rancid. But Dan wasn't inclined to be fussy. It was too early in the evening for the shop to be busy, and in the heated storage compartments under the counter were a pile of chips and some dozen pieces of fish, waiting for customers.

'Tuppenny fish and a penn'orth,' said Dan, feeling affluent.

The slow, bulky woman who was serving looked at him dubiously.

'Got your money, love?' she inquired.

Dan felt in his pocket and carefully separated a single pound note from the rest before bringing it out and offering it. The sight was enough to make the woman stare. A pound was a great deal of money in the Jungle.

'Where d'you get that?' she demanded.

'M-m-my dad gave it me,' Dan said. That was almost true; until a few weeks ago he'd supposed Jack Lunn was his dad.

She gave him a long, searching look.

'All right, I'll take your word for it,' she said at length. 'You've a pathetic face, haven't you, lad? I bet that often gets you out of trouble. Hope I don't have the coppers from across the road coming in here in five minutes' time asking questions about you, that's all.'

Slowly, wrinkling her brow with the effort, she counted out nineteen shillings and ninepence change in greasy silver and copper. There was just enough in the till to complete the transaction. And finally Dan received the hot golden portion, wrapped in newspaper. He shook salt and vinegar over it liberally and began to eat while still in the shop, tearing the fish to pieces with his fingers.

'Anyone'd think you hadn't et for a week,' the woman commented. She still sounded very dubious. 'I hope you *did* come by that money honest.'

'I d-d-did,' Dan assured her between mouthfuls.

His stomach comfortable, Dan set about shopping. It was easier now he had small change. He bought pies and sausage rolls from Dobbs's, the pork butchers, but found he was no longer tempted by the famous ham. He got a loaf of bread from Hassett's, the bakers; margarine and condensed milk and corned beef and a big bottle of lemonade from Simkin's, the grocers; apples and bananas from Trigg's, the greengrocers. A carrier-bag cost him a halfpenny, and he had the forethought to buy a knife and can-opener at the hardware store. He firmly resisted a temptation to buy sweets. Altogether the expedition cost him nearly six shillings.

It was still daylight when he finished. He made his way without incident back to the row of cottages beside the viaduct, and before climbing up to his attic he prowled around the backyards and found the standpipe which Jack had told him of. It was still working. There was also a row of broken-down earth privies, but Dan didn't fancy those. He relieved himself, guiltily, against the brickwork of the viaduct, and resolved to make full use of public conveniences in future. Then, with some difficulty, he got himself and the shopping-bag in through the window.

Home again. Well, at least, it was home for the time being.

CHAPTER 11

Dan unloaded his groceries and arranged them to his satisfaction on the orange-box shelf. There seemed a lot of food there, and when it was finished he could buy more. He took the spare clothes from his satchel and put them into the battered chest of drawers. He placed the photograph of Mum on top of the chest, beside the candle.

Then he peered out of each window in turn through the hole he'd scraped in the grime. At one side he could see a stretch of black canal, with the high walls of factories and warehouses along its farther bank; at the other side were the cleared open spaces that lay on both sides of Canal Street, and beyond them the huddled homes of the Jungle. The third window was the one he'd climbed through and looked only on to the railway viaduct. At each window, a scrap of tattered blanket hung from a hook and could be drawn across to form a primitive curtain.

Dan stretched himself out on the mattress and surveyed his domain. This attic was his own place; he liked it. His stomach was comfortably full. He'd had a long day, and now he could relax and dream a little about the future. Perhaps when his imagined family had become reality he would keep this as a den, known only to him and one or two chosen friends . . .

It was getting dusk now. He heard two or three more trains rumble over the viaduct; he heard St Jude's Church clock strike, but was too sleepy to count the strokes. Then he heard nothing more. He slept through nine, ten and eleven o'clock, and he would have slept through midnight and on into the morning, but a much smaller sound than the Church clock disturbed him. It was a rattle and then a gentle thud at the viaduct end of the room.

Dan jerked upright, instantly wide awake. The attic was now in darkness, except for a faint glimmer from the dirt-encrusted windows. The rattle had been that of the end window, going up. A moving shape briefly filled the window-space; there was a scrabbling sound, followed by a vibration of the floor, as of feet descending on it. Then a pause; yet surely Dan could hear breathing. There was an intruder.

Dan sat, silent, on the mattress, his heart pounding. For a few seconds there was no further sound; then he could hear feet, creeping quietly towards him. He was terrified. This might be the last hour of his life. He could be murdered down here, and it would be days or weeks before anyone knew about it.

Then there was the scratch of a match. Its light showed him a child: a small girl, smaller than himself. He couldn't see anything of her face. The child moved over to the chest of drawers and drew the saucer with the stub of candle towards herself. The match guttered out; she gave a tiny exclamation, then struck another match and held it to the candle. The flame flickered and caught. She picked up the saucer and turned, throwing a little pool of light in front of her. Up to that moment she obviously hadn't been aware of Dan. Now she saw him and started back in fright.

Dan's own fear evaporated rapidly. It was only a small girl. He stood up and called loudly, 'What are you doing?'

The child gave a little cry, quickly suppressed. The saucer shook in her hand; it looked for a moment as if she'd drop it. She put it back on the chest of drawers and turned to face him. She must have been as frightened as he had been a minute earlier, but she was in control of herself.

'It's only me,' she said in a small steady voice.

Dan picked up the candle and held it so he could see her face. It was a sharp, pinched face surrounded by straight fair hair. And in his turn he nearly dropped the candle. There was a big bruise on her cheek and she had a thickly swollen lip.

'W-what's happened to you?' he asked. 'What's *those*?' He pointed to the marks on her face.

'That's Frank,' she said. 'It's nothing. I've had much worse than that.'

'Who's Frank?'

'Just a feller. Lives in the same house.'

'But ... what sort of fellow? Why's he in the same house? What's he been hitting you for?'

The child sounded impatient.

'I told you, it's nothing,' she said. 'Doesn't matter *who* he is, does it? He's three times as big as me, that's *what* he is. He hits me when he's in drink. Other times he's all right.'

'And you've come down here, to a place like this! At this time of night!'

'Well, so would you, if you had Frank after you in one of his tempers. I've been here before, two or three times. Not recently, though.'

'It could be dangerous for a kid like you,' said Dan. He felt surprisingly concerned on her behalf. 'I mean, there might be undesirable characters around.'

'*Frank*'s undesirable,' the child said.

'There's some that could do worse than hit you,' Dan said darkly. Then he saw that her eyes were on the shelf on which he'd put his little store of food. 'Are you hungry?' he asked.

She didn't say anything, but nodded. Dan took the

loaf, hacked off a thick slice, and spread margarine on it. He handed it across to her and she munched steadily but rapidly.

'Another?' he asked. She nodded again. When she'd finished the second slice, her eyes returned to the cut loaf, but it was dwindling and Dan prudently didn't offer her a third. 'What's your name?' he asked.

'Olive.'

'Olive what?'

'Doesn't matter, does it?' she said for the second time.

'How old are you, Olive?'

'Nine, I think. Or ten, maybe.'

'I'm Dan. You planning to sleep here tonight?'

'Yes.'

'Where?'

'Well, I slept on that mattress last time. But I can sleep on the floor. I ain't fussy.'

'There's room for both of us,' Dan said. 'You go that side.'

He was fully dressed except for his boots. Olive had a frock on, but was barefoot. They lay down side by side on the mattress; Dan blew the candle out and drew a blanket over them both. Olive's breathing soon became regular. She seemed to be a matter-of-fact child; neither a beating from Frank nor the trip to this attic and encounter with Dan was enough to keep her awake.

But Dan couldn't get back to sleep. He felt strange; he'd never slept beside another person before. And there was something more than that. Now in the night, in this remote and isolated place, the enormity of what he'd done was striking home to him. He'd left the world he knew and gone out all on his own. How could he have dared?

He tried the old cure for his woes, summoning the imaginary family to his aid. The dad who was not only tall and strong and good-tempered and loving but was now also rich. The Mum who had grown younger and was the photograph come to life: an exquisite young lady in an elegant setting which was permanent and not merely the background for a studio portrait. And himself, secure and parented and friended ...

In the end Dan slept, though he half-woke from time to time, hearing the Church clock or a passing train and becoming aware of the breathing child beside him. Towards morning he found, on one of these half-wakings, that Olive's arms were round his neck, but it wasn't unpleasant and he didn't remove them. Later still, he woke to find that daylight was filtering in through the grimy windows and Olive, out of bed now, was leaning over him and looking with some interest into his face.

'Hello, Dan,' she said. 'It's morning. The sun's shining like anything.'

CHAPTER 12

Dan stood up and shoved the mattress and blankets aside. For a minute he couldn't quite believe that Olive was really there and the events of the night hadn't been part of his dreams. Then, fully awake, he studied her face by daylight. The bruise on her cheek looked nasty.

'Listen,' he said, 'what does this fellow Frank hit you *for*? Is it just because he's drunk?' Dan was recalling that he'd often seen Jack Lunn drunk, but Jack had never touched him.

'He gets bad temper with it,' Olive said patiently. 'He don't mean no harm really. He don't know his own strength, that's Frank's problem. He'll hit me too hard one of these days. Then he'll be in trouble.'

She picked up a fragment of mirror that lay on the chest of drawers, and looked at her face critically. 'He'll be sorry when he sees this,' she said. 'He'll give me something, I dare say. Might be sixpence.'

'But ... who is he, anyway? How d'you come to be in the same house?'

'Oh, I dunno.' She sounded a little bored with the subject. 'There was Walt, then there was lots of fellers, then there was Frank, then him and my mum had a row. You know how it is.'

'And your dad?' Dan asked.

'I don't know anything about him. I musta had one, but it was a long time ago. Before Walt. There's just me and Frank now. And Doug; that's Frank's younger brother. Frank don't want me. Why should he? I'm nothing to him, not really. I told you, he don't mean no harm. He's worse some times than others. I'd sooner be with him than in Broad Street.'

'You know what, Olive?' Dan said. 'You and me got two things in common. We don't know who our dads were and we don't want to be in a home. And another thing, we're both down here in Canal Street. We're a sort of gang, you and me ... Are you hungry again, Olive?'

'Yes, I am. What else you got?' She went over and examined the contents of his store-cupboard. 'Corned beef. I like that.'

Dan opened a can of corned beef and a bottle of lemonade, and they finished the loaf. When they'd eaten, he said, 'You haven't asked about me. Where I come from and all that.'

''s not my business, is it?'

Dan told her all the same. She sat patiently beside him but didn't ask any questions. He finished, 'So I'll be going up to Highwood to find my real dad. I might go tomorrow, seeing it's Sunday. That's a good day for finding people at home. If my dad *is* a Hunter, he's rich!'

'Get away!' she said in a tone of calm disbelief. 'You're making it all up!'

'I'm not!' Dan declared indignantly. He pulled the eleven remaining pound notes out of his pocket. 'This is the money I told you about,' he said. '*Now* do you believe me?'

This time Olive was impressed. She looked at the money with big round eyes. 'That all yours?' she asked. 'You didn't nick it?'

'No, I didn't nick it. You haven't been listening. I told you, it was given to me.'

'Strikes me you don't *need* a rich dad,' she said. 'You're rich already.'

A thin pale shaft of sunshine found its way through a grimy window and showed up the dust that lay everywhere in the attic. Olive surveyed the place with disapproval. 'Could do with cleaning up a bit, couldn't it?' she said.

Dan didn't respond. He wasn't all that interested in cleanliness.

'And look at *you*!' she went on. 'All muck and dust and torn clothes! What's these rich relations of yours going to think of that?'

'I expect when I find my dad,' said Dan, 'I'll get all new clothes to wear.'

She looked him in the eye. 'You really think you're going to find him?' she asked. 'I thought you was just telling the tale. You know, showing off.'

'Well, I'm not!' Dan said indignantly. 'I tell you, the man who was supposed to be my dad told me . . .'

'Some folks'll tell you anything. Still, I'm not saying it ain't true. I dare say things is different for you. I know I'*m* not going to find any rich dad. Or any dad at all, for that matter. There's only Frank.'

'You're going back to him, then?'

''Course I am. Where else would I go? I shan't go back today, though. It's Sat'day, he'll be drunk again tonight. I'll give him the weekend to cool down. Monday, he'll be broke and sorry. And now, pass me that brush over there and you take the shovel and we'll tidy up a bit.'

'Here, who are you bossing around?' Dan demanded.

Dan had half a mind to be cross, but she was grinning at him in a friendly way, and he hadn't the heart.

'Of course, when you're in a big house at Highwood you'll have servants to do all the work,' she said, 'but there ain't no servants down here in Canal Street. So get on with it.'

Dan grinned back and got on with it. A few minutes later, shifting the chest of drawers in the corner of the attic, he noticed something about the floorboards.

'Here, Olive,' he said, 'there's something funny about this. The floor's sort of cut across.'

She came and looked. And even as he spoke, Dan realized what he was looking at. Half-hidden under ancient dirt, and barely visible anyway in its dark corner, was a trap-door. With a good deal of effort they levered it up, and a few minutes later were peering through the opening into the filthy deserted bedroom of the end cottage underneath.

'It'd be handy if we could get up and down through here,' Dan said. He hadn't liked climbing on the outside wall. 'But I don't see how we'd do it. We'd need a ladder.'

'We won't find no ladder, that's for sure. But look, Dan. We're right over the alcove alongside the chimney, right? There's been a shelf across that alcove some time, hasn't there? You can see the supports it rested on. Now suppose that shelf was still there, you could lower yourself on to it dead easy from here. Then you'd get from the shelf to the mantelpiece; it's plenty broad enough. And from that you could jump down.'

'And what if you were coming up instead?'

'Well, it'd help if you had a box or something to stand on, to get on to the mantelpiece. But it'd be easy from then on. Mantelpiece to shelf, then push up the trap from below and Bob's your uncle.'

'It'd need to be a good strong shelf,' said Dan doubtfully.

'Well, let's see what we can find,' she said.

They were in luck. In the outhouse where the standpipe was, there was also a good deal of lumber. They found a stout plank which would form a shelf across the alcove and only needed cutting to size.

'This is where we start spending some of your money, Dan,' said Olive. 'Got that bit of pencil? We'll make a shopping list. Write down what I say. We want a good saw to cut that plank to size. And we need a bucket and a scrubbing-brush and some carbolic soap and a towel. And some needles and thread, for your clothes. And listen, Dan, there's no need to live on bully beef and sardines, we can buy a primus stove – they don't cost all that much – and a pan, and then we can cook. And while we're out we can get some spuds – they're cheapest at Handley's – and carrots, and some stewing steak, and that's our dinner. And then . . .'

'Hold on a minute!' Dan said. 'You're saying 'em faster than I can write them down. And do we really want all that stuff? We'll only be here a day or two, most likely.'

She looked crestfallen, but only for a moment. Then she said, 'Well, we can make it nice anyway. We might come back some time, who knows?'

By mid-afternoon the shopping was done, the shelf made and tested and found to take their weight, and they were on their knees scrubbing the floor. When they'd finished, the attic was a good deal cleaner than they were themselves. Dan went for more water. They washed their faces, splashing each other happily, and dried themselves on the new towel.

'I like it here, Dan,' said Olive. 'The place where I live with Frank isn't much better, and I can't keep it nice with him around. And getting money from him for soap and so on is like getting blood out of a stone. Frank don't hand the money out like you do . . . Which reminds me. How much you got left, Dan?'

'Just over ten pounds.'

'You want to take care of that. It's a lot of money. If you carry it around you might lose it or get it nicked or anything.'

'I could hide most of it here,' said Dan. 'There's lots of hiding-places.'

They looked around for somewhere to conceal the money. Eventually they tucked the folded notes in the space behind a rafter in a dark corner.

'That's fine,' said Olive with approval. She looked around at the results of their cleaning. 'We've made a difference this morning, haven't we, pal?'

Dan felt curiously happy. 'You know, I never really had a pal,' he said. 'I mean, I knew them all at school, but they never came home with me or anything like that.'

'I never had nobody much either,' she said. 'This feels as if it's really our place, doesn't it?'

'Listen,' said Dan. 'When I find my dad, what if I ask him to adopt you?'

'Who're you kidding?'

'Well, he might, you never know.' Dan's imaginary family had always included a younger sister. True, he'd thought of her as a tiny girl, riding on her father's shoulders. But there was no reason why she shouldn't be Olive's age. 'The Hunters have lots and lots of money,' he said. 'They could afford to adopt anybody they liked.'

'Don't be daft, Dan. I can tell you one thing right away. They wouldn't adopt *me*. Nobody wants a kid from the Shambles.'

'The Shambles!' Dan repeated. 'You come from the *Shambles*!'

He was startled. The Jungle was the worst part of the city, and the Shambles was the worst part of the Jungle. It was across the railway tracks, down by the canal basin: the lowest of low areas. Respectable parents didn't let their children mix with riff-raff from the Shambles.

Dan considered how Hilda and Aunt Verity would have recoiled in horror at the very idea. Then he was surprised to hear his own voice saying out loud, 'I can't see that it matters.'

'It does, you know,' she said. 'Oh well, seeing we've taken so much trouble we may as well enjoy ourselves while we're here. I'm going to make us a meal for tonight, Dan; a real nice meal.'

CHAPTER 13

Dan woke next morning to hear the bells of half a dozen churches calling people to early service. Olive was up before him, making porridge in their one saucepan.

'You still planning to look for your posh relations?' she inquired.

'Yes, I am,' he said. 'But don't worry, I won't just stay with them and leave you, without saying anything. I'll tell you what happens.'

'Thanks a lot,' she said drily. 'Then I can go back to Frank.'

Half an hour later Dan set off, full of high resolve. At

the junction of Hibiscus Street with Camellia Hill, he boarded the tramcar. The half fare to Highwood from here was three halfpence. Dan paid, went upstairs, and sat in the high, curved prow of the tram as it groaned its way up the long, slow hill. It passed the endless small shops, the endless rows of houses that grew gradually more respectable as the ascent continued. People in Sunday best got on and off.

Beyond the Chrysanthemums the houses thinned out. On the right was the city park, on the left the cemetery. Then on both sides there were glimpses of country. And finally the tramcar, gathering speed, soared on its last triumphant flight to the splendours of Highwood.

You couldn't even *see* the city from Highwood; a shoulder of the hill was in the way. Highwood had turned its back on the source of its wealth; it looked instead towards the dales, and beyond them, faint and violet and hazy, the chain of high hills that had been called the backbone of England.

The sun was shining when the tram arrived at the Highwood terminus: a square of green across which a couple of imposing pubs faced each other. Dan was the last passenger to leave. The conductor twiddled a handle to change the destination indicator so that it said CITY instead of HIGHWOOD, then turned the overhead trolley-bar in readiness for the tram's return journey.

Dan looked for someone who could help him to find the Hunters. At first there was nobody around. The tram had left the terminus, heading back into town, before a middle-aged lady came along. She wore a severe grey suit and a velour hat, and was pushing a perambulator. Dan had some difficulty in summoning up the courage to approach her. But she looked kindly.

'Hunters?' she said. 'Of course I know the Hunters. They're next door to *my* family. Just come along with me.'

It was quite a long walk, along a broad, tree-lined avenue, past ten or a dozen large grey stone houses, all surrounded by huge smooth lawns and carefully tended flowerbeds. Dan's guide chatted pleasantly to him as they went. He learned that she was a nannie, employed by the Winterton family: 'Winterton's fabrics, you know.' The baby's name was Emily and she was a little dear, though her brother Charles was a handful. And what was Dan expecting to do at the Hunters'?

Dan didn't think it tactful to explain his quest. He managed to imply without actually lying that he was hoping to find part-time work in the house or garden. The nannie seemed to think his chances slight, but wished him well. 'This is where my family live,' she said eventually. 'Keep straight on and you'll come to the Hunters', next on this side. Good luck.' And she turned away into a wide gravel drive, leaving Dan to complete the last lap on his own.

The Hunters' house was the most imposing of all. Its grounds were surrounded by a high stone wall. Peering through an enormous main gate made of wrought iron, Dan could see a broad drive leading through an expanse of lawn to the front portico of a handsome, foursquare, stone-built mansion. Before the portico stood a large, stately motorcar. Just inside the gate was a lodge, with a thread of smoke rising from its chimney. There was a bell beside the gate, but Dan wouldn't have dared to ring it.

For a short while, Dan was dismayed. He hadn't expected anything quite so grand as this. How could he bring himself to the notice of people who lived in such splendour? Probably he wouldn't even get to see them. But there was a dogged streak in Dan. He wasn't going to give up at this stage. And why should he be daunted? In Grandpa's storybooks a transition from rags to riches was commonplace. One of the heroes, a poor boy living in a shoemaker's family, had turned out to be a rightful earl, no less. True, this boy had had an aristocratic radiance, shining through his rags, which no one had ever noticed in Dan. On the other hand, Dan wasn't expecting to rise as high as an earldom . . . He would stick to his plan. But he couldn't bring himself to ring that bell. He walked farther along the outside of the wall, and came to a much smaller wooden side-gate on which were the words TRADESMEN'S ENTRANCE.

Dan raised the latch, pushed, and found that the gate was open. Inside it, a gravel path led round through a grove of trees towards the rear quarters of the main house. Heart bumping, he slipped through the gate and closed it behind him. There was plenty of cover among the trees. He left the path and dived under the spreading branches of a great beech. From here he had a sideways view of the huge front lawn, the house, and the motorcar still parked in front of the portico.

He could now see that there was a chauffeur at the wheel of the car, reading a newspaper. And as he watched, the front door of the house opened and a youngish gentleman, in overcoat and bowler hat, came down the steps. He was giving his arm to a much older lady in a fur coat. The chauffeur, hastily putting down his newspaper, jumped from the motorcar and held its back door open.

The gentleman handed the lady with some care into the car and got in beside her. The chauffeur resumed his seat and the car drew slowly, impressively away down the drive. As it approached the main gate it hooted and a man appeared from the lodge, opened the gate and stood beside it until the car had gone. He went back into the lodge, and the grounds were silent and empty in Sunday morning calm. No further sign of movement came from the house.

Dan stayed where he was under the beech-tree. He was adjusting his daydream. The gentleman was obviously Mr Hunter, and the lady must be his mother. Mr Hunter – in Dan's dream – was indeed the missing dad, but didn't yet know of Dan's existence. Mum, loyal and loving, had never even told him, for fear of the embarrassment she would cause. Mr Hunter didn't know where she was; didn't even know that she was alive. When he found he had a son, his life would change completely. He would seek Mum out and marry her. Mr Hunter's own mother would be delighted to find she had a grandchild. There was of course the minor difficulty that Mum was married already to Jack Lunn, but rich people knew how to deal with such matters. In very little time they would all be installed here, a happy family . . .

'Gotcher!' said a male voice, and Dan felt a fierce grip on his arm. He turned to find himself captured by a tall, lean lad of some sixteen or seventeen years, with curly blond hair.

'What you up to?' the lad demanded; and then, without waiting for an answer, 'You come with me!'

Dan had no choice. The lad dragged him to the path and round to the back of the house. 'Fred!' he yelled. 'Fred!'

A bent elderly man with a weatherworn face emerged from the door of an outbuilding. He looked annoyed.

'What you mean, shouting like that on a Sunday morning?' he demanded. And then, 'Who's the lad?'

'I found him hiding under the beech-tree.'

Fred walked round Dan, inspecting him with some care from all angles. Then he asked, 'Is that right?'

Dan nodded.

'What was you doing there?'

Dan was silent. He couldn't bring himself to tell this old man of his mission.

'Go on, lad. Answer me. You're not dumb, are you? You can see these is private grounds. What was you up to, hiding?'

'N-nothing,' Dan said with an effort.

'You don't have to come in here to do *nowt*,' the old man said. 'You can do nowt anywhere. You must have been doing *summat*!'

'I j-just wanted to watch them get in the car,' Dan said feebly.

A couple of maids had come out of a side door of the house and were watching with interest. One of them said, 'Mr Daniel and Lady Hunter just left for church. The car went down the drive a few minutes ago.'

'What's that to do wi' you?' the old man asked Dan. But Dan couldn't answer. He was full of excitement over what he'd just heard.

'*What* did you say his name was?' he demanded, the stammer suddenly overcome.

'Mr Daniel? That's Mr Daniel Hunter, of course. We allus call him Mr Daniel here. Lady Hunter's his mum. His dad was Sir Richard, but he's dead. And now, young feller, answer my question. What's it to do with you?'

Dan forgot himself, forgot caution, forgot everything, and burst out, 'He might be my dad!'

There was a startled silence. Dan realized what he'd said, and shrank into himself. He looked apprehensively from one face to another. The curly-haired boy pointed a finger significantly at the side of his head. The old man said, 'Are you barmy, lad? Are you out of Ridwell?'

Ridwell was the mental institution a few miles away. Dan shook his head vigorously.

'Well, either you're daft or you're up to summat funny,' the old man declared with conviction. 'What's your name?'

'Daniel Hunter Lunn.'

There was a second startled silence. Then Fred said,

'Better send for Mrs Donaldson.' One of the maids disappeared. The other giggled. 'Looks a bit like him, don't he?' she said. 'They both have big ears!' The curly boy guffawed. Fred told them both to be quiet.

Mrs Donaldson, solid and middle-aged, was clearly a person of some importance in the household. In her turn she looked Dan up and down. Then she said solemnly, 'Tell me your name, boy. Your real name.'

'D-daniel Hunter Lunn.'

'Is this some joke?'

'N-no, ma'am. It's my real name. It is, truly.'

'He says Mr Daniel's his dad!' put in the curly boy with relish.

'I d-d-didn't say he *is* my dad. I only th-thought he might be.'

'You are suggesting . . .' Mrs Donaldson dropped her voice, in mingled outrage and embarrassment. 'You are surely not suggesting . . .' Her voice dropped farther, until it was hardly more than a whisper. 'You are not claiming an *illegitimate relationship* with Mr Daniel Hunter?'

The maid who had giggled before giggled again. Mrs Donaldson packed her off sharply to her work. Dan stood tongue-tied.

'I reckon the lad's soft in the head,' said Fred. 'We could hand him over to the police, for loitering. But if you ask me, we should just throw him out.'

'I did not ask you, Mr Stone,' said Mrs Donaldson coldly. 'This is not your province. *I* shall decide what to do.'

'All right, Mrs D,' said Fred. 'I'm only the gardener. Sorry I spoke.'

Mrs Donaldson said, half to herself, 'I think it would be better not to involve the police. One doesn't know quite what the child might tell them.' And then, decisively, to Dan: 'You had better see Mr Daniel. This sounds to me like a very wicked story you're telling. But it's for him to send you packing, not me. You will wait in my room until he returns from church.'

Mrs Donaldson turned to the curly-haired boy. 'Alan, take him to the housekeeper's room and stay there with him until he's sent for.' She added with distaste, 'I hope he's clean.'

A minute later Dan was sitting in a small cosy room at the back of the house. Alan sat beside him, his eyes bright with interest.

'Are you *really* his?' he inquired hopefully. 'We all know he's fond of the lasses, but I'd never have thought ...' A pause. 'You're not much like him, are you?' Another pause; then, in the tones of one dismissing an attractive possibility, ''*Course* you're not his. You're barmy, aren't you? Straight out of Ridwell! Well, you're in trouble now. If you're not back in Ridwell, you'll be in jail, I wouldn't wonder!'

Dan sat still and said nothing. He was going to see Mr Hunter, which was what he'd wanted. He ought to have been overjoyed. But he wasn't. He'd had a vague mental picture of himself running into the welcoming arms of a long-lost father; but he was beginning to suspect that it wouldn't be like that at all.

CHAPTER 14

It was a long half-hour before Mrs Donaldson re-appeared.

'Come this way, lad,' she said grimly. 'Mr Daniel will see you in the drawing-room. I'd have thought myself he'd want to see you in private, if at all. But he told me, he's nothing to hide; you can say what you have to say in front of Her Ladyship and Miss Pitts.'

Dan shivered. He was frightened now. He followed Mrs Donaldson along narrow passages, through a doorway hung with green baize, and into a huge, marble-floored hall, shiny and slippery. From this hall opened the great double front doors of the house, while a broad shallow staircase led to a galleried first floor. Mrs Donaldson's shoes clacked ahead of him across the hall. She tapped at a door, opened it and pushed Dan inside.

'The boy,' she announced, and withdrew.

There were three people in the room: the youngish gentleman, who was obviously Mr Daniel; the older lady, who no doubt was his mother, Lady Hunter; and a smart, saucy-faced young lady with short hair, a boyish figure and a very short skirt. The room itself was high and handsome, but Dan had no eyes for its furnishings or for the view from its great bay windows. He advanced hesitantly across the floor. Mr Daniel and the young lady looked highly amused, but Lady Hunter didn't look amused at all.

'Well, well!' said Mr Daniel. 'So this is our young relative!'

He had a fresh, almost ruddy complexion and brown wavy hair, but he wasn't quite so young as he appeared at first sight. There were crow's-feet at the corners of his eyes and the first signs of greyness in his hair, and he was thickening noticeably at the waist. His voice was hearty but his eyes were sharp.

'Tell us your name, lad,' he invited.

Dan struggled and got it out: 'D-d-daniel Hunter Lunn.'

Mr Daniel laughed.

'Very good,' he said. 'Now tell us your real name.'

'It *is* my real name.'

86

'We'll leave that aside for the moment,' said Mr Daniel. 'What have you come here for?'

Dan was silent, trying to summon up courage.

'Go on, don't be afraid. You must have plenty of cheek to be here at all.'

'I th-thought you might be my dad.'

'Splendid!' said Mr Daniel. 'That's what Mrs Donaldson *said* you said. Well, you've certainly given the servants something to talk about.'

Miss Pitts said, 'Is this your past coming to light, darling?' She and Mr Daniel both laughed.

Lady Hunter didn't join in the laughter. She said to Dan, 'I don't know whether you understand what you're saying, but it is very wicked.'

'There, there, Mother,' said Mr Daniel. 'You're not taking this seriously, are you? I assure you, to the best of my knowledge and belief you are not a grandmother.'

'That remark is not funny,' said Lady Hunter coldly.

Mr Daniel's eyes narrowed and he looked less jovial.

'Somebody's put you up to this, haven't they, lad?' he said. 'Who was it?'

'Nobody put me up to it,' Dan said; and then, pulling the photograph from his pocket, 'This is my mum.'

Mr Daniel took the picture from him. Miss Pitts moved to his side to look at it. Lady Hunter stayed where she was.

'Pretty, isn't she?' said Miss Pitts, and added mischievously, 'Are you *sure* there isn't some little incident you've forgotten, dearest? Shouldn't you tell me now, rather than after we're married?'

'Really, Veronica!' said Lady Hunter.

Mr Daniel handed the photograph back to Dan.

'I have never seen this lady in my life,' he said. His voice sharpened. 'Now, lad, whoever you really are. Go back to the person who sent you. Tell him there's nothing doing. If this is some kind of blackmail attempt, it won't wash. Nobody's going to get a penny out of me with a trumped-up story like that. If you show your face here again, it'll be straight to the police station with you, understand? And the same goes for whoever put you up to it, right?'

Lady Hunter now seemed more sympathetic than her son.

'Sending a child like that on such an errand!' she exclaimed. 'Whoever did it deserves to be found and sent to prison!' She added thoughtfully, 'And yet ... he doesn't look a *bad* boy, does he?'

'He certainly has a pathetic expression,' said Miss Pitts.

'The innocent-looking ones are the worst,' said Mr Daniel. 'It's their stock-in-trade.' He turned to Dan. 'I hope that's clear to you, lad: nothing doing. Now I'm going to have you put out on the road to town with a boot in your backside.'

'Daniel!' said Lady Hunter, in a tone of mild protest.

'He's asked for it, Mother,' said Mr Daniel. 'But if he prefers, I'll call the police now.' Again he turned to Dan. 'Would you rather I did that, eh?'

Dan was trembling, but with an enormous effort he pulled himself together. He had made up his mind about Mr Daniel.

'I'll go,' he said; and then, with dignity, 'It's all right, Mr Hunter. I can tell you're not my dad. I don't *want* you for my dad. Thank you very much.'

Mr Daniel stared at him. For a moment he seemed taken aback. Then he rang the bell. Mrs Donaldson reappeared with great promptitude.

'Have this lad put outside,' said Mr Daniel.

CHAPTER 15

The same tramcar was waiting at the Highwood terminus. It had journeyed into town and out again during
Dan's visit to the Hunters. He boarded it despondently
and it clanged its way into the city, picking up passen-
gers at every stop until it was crowded. Dan sat squashed
into a corner, surrounded by people yet feeling more
alone than he'd ever felt in his life.

His dream had collapsed completely. He tried to put it
together again in a new setting, totally unlike Highwood,
with a new dad, totally unlike Mr Daniel. But it wouldn't
work any more. He couldn't have put it into words, but
at last he knew the dream for what it was: a deception.
There was only the real world to live in.

He toyed with the thought of staying in the attic where
he and Olive had made their temporary home. But once
reality had broken in there was no keeping it out. He
couldn't live on his own for long. Jack Lunn's money
would be spent and winter would come. There was
nothing he could do but pick up his few possessions and
the money, and hand himself over to the mercy of his
relatives. And yet . . . what about Olive? She would go
back to Frank, of course, but . . . Dan was still wondering
what would happen to Olive when the tram reached the
junction of Camellia Hill and Hibiscus Street. He got off.
And a moment later a voice was calling him.

'Dan! Danny! Dan Lunn!'

Dan looked round, alarmed. The tall thin figure of
Benjy the glazier was bearing down on him. He felt a
strong impulse to run. If he'd been with Mum she would

89

have turned pointedly away; the man would have crossed the street and silently watched them go by on the other side. But he wasn't with Mum, and the man wasn't silent.

'Danny! I want to talk to you!'

Dan ignored the man and walked rapidly downhill without speaking. The glazier caught up and walked beside him, his long strides out of rhythm with Dan's shorter ones.

'Danny!' he repeated. 'Danny, listen!'

Dan looked up at the pale, bearded face, the anxious brown eyes, and shuddered. He had always feared the glazier; he still feared him. But there didn't seem any way of shaking him off. If he ran, people might think he'd stolen something.

They continued all the way down Hibiscus Street. At the corner of Canal Street Dan stopped; he didn't want the man going with him to his secret place.

The glazier put both hands on his shoulders, not fiercely but making him wince with apprehension. Then the man was shaken by a fit of coughing. He released Dan for long enough to put a large white handkerchief to his mouth. Dan could have broken away, but stayed where he was, alarmed.

The coughing ceased. Gasping, the man said, 'Danny, what's happened to your mum?'

Dan kept his lips tightly closed.

'The house has been sold, hasn't it?' Benjy went on. 'Where is she now?'

'I d-d-don't know.'

'You're not with her, then?'

Dan shook his head, silently. Tears were coming to his eyes, but he fought against them. No, he wasn't with his mother and he didn't know where she was.

'You've been at your grandpa's?'

A nod from Dan.

'I thought so. But *she's* not been there ... What you going to do when your grandpa dies?'

Dan jumped. 'He might not die,' he said.

'It looks bad, Danny. The doctor's there now, or was a few minutes ago. I saw Mrs Lester from next door, and she told me. Your grandpa was singing hymns, she said, all last night and this morning. They told him he'd tire himself out, singing all them hymns for all he was worth, but he wouldn't take no notice, just sang and sang. And then he had another attack. Nobody can see him now.'

The glazier was overcome by another fit of coughing. Dan gulped hard, still determined not to cry. The man recovered and went on, 'I'm sorry I had to tell you, lad. But you better be prepared. I suppose you and Hilda Selby'll be company for each other. Or will you be going to your auntie's?'

It occurred to Dan that the glazier knew a good deal about his affairs. He resented it and didn't answer.

'Let me walk you back to whichever of them you're staying with,' the man suggested.

Dan felt himself going out of control and almost shouting, 'You mind your own business!'

The glazier said thoughtfully, 'Maybe you don't like it much, living with either of them.' He paused, then added, 'Of course, if your grandpa passed away, that'd be a big change. I wish *I* could give you a home, Danny.'

'*You*!' Dan was astonished.

'Yes. Trouble is, I don't have a settled place. I live where I can. Just now, I got a room in the Poppies, but that's only for a week or two. After that it might be an outhouse, a shed, a stable, anything. Or it might be another room if I'm lucky. You see, Danny, there's no money in what I do. Sometimes I feel tempted to break a few windows myself, to give me a bit of business.' Benjy smiled wearily, as if at a joke many times made. 'But I

91

live. If the worst came to the worst, I'd do my best for you.'

Dan was appalled. He looked up at the gaunt figure of the glazier, remembering his mother's fear of the man, and wondering why Benjy should take such an interest and what horrors might lie in wait if he delivered himself over to such a person. Even Aunt Verity, even Hilda, even the orphanage, would be preferable to that.

Benjy's hands were still resting lightly on his shoulders, not gripping. At the moment there was no one around. Dan broke away and ran: ran at top speed. The sound of his boots echoed from the pavement. After half a minute he looked back. The glazier had followed him a little way, but now he had come to a halt and was leaning against a wall, coughing. He wasn't going to catch him, or see where he went.

Dan had doubled back along Hibiscus Street. Now he cut through into Canal Street, where he slowed down and walked sedately all the way to the row of cottages beside the viaduct. As usual he looked around warily; as usual there was no one to be seen. He went into the end cottage, climbed up to the trap-door and hauled himself through it.

'Olive!' he called. 'Olive!'

There was no reply at first. Then her voice came feebly, 'Dan!'

She was lying on the mattress with a blanket drawn over her.

'Olive! What's up?'

'I'm not feeling all that well, Dan.'

Dan knelt on the boards beside her, alarmed. He couldn't see her face clearly in the poor light. 'What *sort* of not well?' he asked.

'Feel my forehead.' She took his hand and put it on her brow, which was hot and dry. 'A minute ago I was shivering.'

'It's come on suddenly, hasn't it?'

'Yes, well, I wasn't feeling up to much when we got up this morning, but I didn't say anything. And then just after you'd gone out it really hit me. Nearly knocked me over. I got a splitting head and all sort of aches and pains. And weak, I'm as weak as a kitten. I don't think I could get up off here if I tried.'

'You're hoarse.'

'Yes, I got a sore throat, too.'

'Let's have a proper look at you,' Dan said. He reached for the candle and lit it.

'It hurts my eyes,' she said. 'Anyway, there's nothing to see.'

Dan sat beside her on the mattress. He was seriously alarmed. Most of Grandpa's books had a chapter – some had two or three – in which a child was smitten with a fever. Usually the victim would become delirious and ramble incoherently. A doctor would come, shake his head and predict the worst. Watch would be kept on the bedside night and day. The fever would intensify. All hope would be abandoned. Then, usually, the crisis would pass, and one day the patient would wake up, weak but clear-headed and on the way to recovery. Sometimes however there was no recovery; the family would gather round, the sufferer would breathe his or her last, the blinds would be drawn down, and the next chapter would be devoted to the funeral.

'What you thinking about?' Olive asked.

'I was thinking a doctor ought to see you.'

'Don't be daft, Dan!' she said. 'I got flu, that's what it is. Frank's younger brother Doug had it the other week. It won't kill me, no more'n it killed him.'

'Well, maybe I should bring Frank. He might want to call the doctor.'

'Frank won't pay for a doctor, I can tell you that. He don't have no patience with illness. He'd have me cooking and cleaning as usual. I'm better off here, Danny. That's if you can put up with me.' She reached for his hand.

''Course I can put up with you,' Dan said. 'What do I have to do?'

'You can get me a drink of water, I'm so thirsty you wouldn't believe. And you can go to the chemist's for some aspirin. And you can keep your face away from mine, or you'll be getting it too. And, Danny . . .'

'Yes, Olive?'

'You're a good lad,' she said, and shivered.

CHAPTER 16

Dan spent the next three days looking after Olive. She had been quite right in saying she had influenza, and for some time after his return from Highwood it got worse. In spite of the aspirins he bought, her headache and the pains in her limbs grew more acute. She tossed and turned at night, and for hours couldn't sleep; then, more distressing for Dan, moaned as she slept. She felt light-headed, had a sore throat and pains around her eyes; she was constantly thirsty but couldn't eat anything. But she grinned feebly at Dan whenever he came near her, and assured him that Doug had been every bit as bad.

On Tuesday her forehead became hot and moist and she sweated heavily. This would have alarmed Dan as much as the earlier symptoms, but she told him it meant she was getting better. And again she was right. By Wednesday morning she was sitting up, still complaining of weakness but clearly on the mend. Dan, who'd been living on whatever food there happened to be in the orange-box cupboard, told her it was time she had something to eat. She wasn't hungry, and her throat was still sore, but after some discussion Dan went out and bought bread and milk. He fed her on sops of bread, soaked in the warmed milk.

'Time I was up and doing, Dan Lunn,' she said.

But when she tried to get up from the mattress she was almost too weak to stand. She flopped back in some surprise. 'Maybe later on I'll manage,' she told him; and then, 'Hey, Danny! You never told me what happened up at Highwood!'

Dan told her. She didn't seem surprised by the outcome.

'And I had a fright on the way back,' he said. 'The Jew-boy caught me. But I got away.'

'The Jew-boy?'

'You know. The man that mends windows. Benjy.'

'Oh, Benjy. I know Benjy. 'Course I know Benjy. But what do you mean, Benjy *caught* you? He wouldn't hurt a fly.'

Dan stared. 'The kids are all scared of him,' he said. 'And lots of grown-ups, too. I reckon even my mum was scared of him.'

Olive's voice had been feeble, but now it strengthened. 'Listen here, Dan Lunn,' she said. 'Benjy's all right. He's a pal of mine.'

'A *pal* of yours!' Dan was shocked. Some of Grandpa's prejudices were deeply ingrained in him. 'How did a fellow like that come to be a pal of yours?'

'Oh, there were some kids in the Shambles chucking half-bricks at him, and I sort of got in the way. It wasn't anything. But we been pals ever since. Benjy never did nobody any harm.'

'Then why are they all afraid of him?' Dan demanded.

'It's because he's a Jew, that's all. Though as a matter

of fact he doesn't observe, or whatever it is they're supposed to do. He got into trouble with his own people a
long time ago – something to do with a girl that wasn't
Jewish, I think – and they fell out with him, or him with
them, I don't know which. Anyway, he's on his own
now. Like me, except for Frank. Maybe that's why we're
pals.'

'Like me, too,' said Dan in some surprise.

'So next time you see Benjy, don't run away. Tell him
you're a friend of mine. He's a *kind* feller, Dan, he is truly,
but nobody'll let him be what he really is, they just think
he's the Jew-boy and they run off or heave a brick at him
or look the other way.'

'Oh,' said Dan. After years of fearing the glazier he
couldn't quite take this in. 'Well . . .'

'Anyway, Dan, seeing you ain't got a rich dad after all,
what you going to do now?'

Dan had had time to think about this. 'There's just one
of my lot that I can get on with,' he said, 'and that's my
Uncle Bert. He's not a real uncle, he's my Aunt Verity's
husband. If I could get him on his own, I wouldn't mind
talking to him about what to do.'

'How'll you get him on his own?'

'It might not be too hard. He's a traveller in dog-
biscuits. Goes round shops. Well, Thursday's early
closing day around here, so he has it as *his* half-day. And
he'll be in the club, a few streets from where he lives,
playing billiards. He does it every week, regular.'

'You better go and see him tomorrow then, Danny.
And the day after that I'll go back to Frank. He'll be
thinking he's got rid of me if I don't go back soon.'

'Do you *have* to?'

'Have a bit of sense, lad. What else would I do? Anyway, I've told you, Frank's not so bad except when he's
drunk, and then I keep out of his way. It's not like being
with you, Danny pal, but that ain't possible, is it? And

now . . . I'm so tired after a bit of talking, anybody'd think I'd been scrubbing floors all morning.'

'You need more rest,' said Dan. 'You'd better stay in bed today.'

'Getting bossy, aren't you, Dan Lunn? I'll be up and out tomorrow, I'm telling you. But just for now, just to please you . . .'

'That's right,' said Dan, and drew the blanket over her.

Dan had gone into and out of the row of cottages half a dozen times and never seen anyone in the deserted open spaces that stretched up to Canal Street and beyond. On Thursday afternoon, he glanced around, expecting to find the coast clear as usual, before setting off to find Uncle Bert. But he'd barely put a foot outside when he glimpsed movement under the arches of the railway viaduct. He darted back into shelter. Somebody was hanging around. And it was a person he knew; the tall, narrow-eyed boy who had been leader of the gang that ambushed him in the Jungle.

Dan peered out cautiously. Narrow-Eyes had been forced by Leo to give up his prey. Dan didn't want to fall into his hands again. Luckily the boy showed no sign of having seen him. He lingered for some time, during which Dan didn't dare to venture outside. It seemed most likely that he was waiting for somebody. Eventually he appeared to give up; he came out from under the arches and walked briskly away along Canal Street with no more than a passing glance at the row of cottages.

Dan gave him plenty of time to get clear. He was a little disturbed. Narrow-Eyes was the first person he'd seen down here, except, of course, Olive.

The working men's club to which Uncle Bert belonged was farther up the hill than the Daisies and Marigolds: almost as far out of town as the city cemetery. At the corner of the main road with Marigold Grove, a cluster of people blocked the pavement. They were watching something, and showed no sign of moving out of the way. As Dan picked his way gently between them, he felt a tap on his shoulder.

'Off with your cap, lad!' said an elderly man just beside him. A funeral procession was just emerging from the side-street into City Hill. It was headed by a large, square motor-hearse carrying a coffin entirely covered with flowers. Behind it crawled, at a slow walking pace, two more black cars; and following them was a long straggling crocodile of people on foot.

For a moment, Dan's mind registered only that there was a funeral. Processions like this were a commonplace, here on the road to the cemetery. He had seen scores of them. Half-consciously he noted that the second car behind the motor-hearse was a black Crossley like Uncle Bert's.

Then it sank in. The car wasn't *like* Uncle Bert's Crossley. It *was* Uncle Bert's Crossley, and Uncle Bert himself was at the wheel.

This was Grandpa's funeral.

It wasn't a surprise, of course; far from it; yet Dan felt weak-kneed with shock. During Olive's illness he'd somehow managed not to think of Grandpa; and now Grandpa was dead.

In the back of the first car, side by side, sat Aunt Verity and Hilda, both in black and wearing black hats with veils. Hilda, veil pushed aside, was mopping her eyes. Uncle Bert's car held two or three distant cousins whom Dan hardly knew. Mum was not there. The procession seemed to contain the whole congregation of the Chapel and half the population of the streets around. The men were hatless, with bowed heads and grave expressions; many of the women were weeping.

'A well-respected man, was Percy Purvis,' said the

man who'd tapped on Dan's shoulder. 'You can tell that from the turnout. He'd have rejoiced to see it.'

'He only passed away on Sunday, didn't he?' said another elderly man beside him.

'They bury them prompt, this time of year,' the first man told him. He added, 'I'm told there'll be fifty at the tea in the Chapel rooms afterwards. Everything done in style!'

'He'll be missed at the Chapel,' the second man said. 'They don't make men like Percy any more.'

The end of the procession tailed away up the hill. The men on the pavement replaced their hats, the traffic flowed again, and the street resumed its normal activities. Dan wondered for a moment whether he should follow the mourners to the cemetery, to see the coffin carried to the grave and the Reverend John Railton conduct the burial service. But, quite apart from the risk of being seen, he didn't want to do so. Grandpa had bidden him farewell and had said he was content. That was good. Nothing Dan could do now mattered in the least.

The sun was shining. There was no hope of consulting Uncle Bert this afternoon. Dan walked, dry-eyed, to the patch of ground known as the Edge, and lay face down on the summer grass. After a while his tightly clenched feelings began to relax and he wept: a little for Grandpa but more for Mum and himself. When he had wept enough, he went to sleep. Later in the afternoon he woke up and remembered Olive, and wondered how she was.

CHAPTER 17

Remembering his sighting of Narrow-Eyes, Dan kept a special lookout as he returned along Canal Street towards the railway viaduct. In addition he went and peered cautiously under the arches. But there was no sign of anyone. On impulse he decided to re-enter the attic as he'd done before finding the trap-door. He climbed the drainpipe, sidestepped, lifted the window sash and slid inside.

'Hello!' he called. 'Olive! How are you?'

There was no reply. And as his eyes became adjusted to the gloom he saw that she wasn't there.

There was nowhere in the attic to hide. She must have gone out. But she hadn't said she was going out. She hadn't seemed fit to go out.

Probably she'd be back soon. Dan sprawled on the mattress. He had plenty to think about. His mind whirled restlessly around: from Grandpa to Hilda to Aunt Verity to Uncle Bert to Basil to Mum to Jack Lunn to the Hunters to the Jewish glazier to Narrow-Eyes and back to Olive ... Time passed, but she didn't return.

She must have gone back to Frank.

Dan told himself that was just as well. She was off his hands. He didn't have to worry about her any more. And yet ... he didn't feel relieved by that thought. He'd got used to Olive. She belonged here. He wished he knew for sure what had happened to her.

It was when St Jude's clock struck six that he suddenly realized he was hungry. In fact he was famished. He hadn't eaten all day, and during Olive's illness the orange-box shelves had been emptied of food.

Well, at least that needn't be a problem. He still had plenty of money. He got up, went over to the roof-beam, and felt behind it.

The money wasn't there.

Perhaps he wasn't looking in the right place. Dan checked behind adjoining beams and looked on the floor beneath, but there was still nothing. He felt a rising panic. He hunted all over the attic, including places where it couldn't possibly have been, and checked the same spots over and over again, as if by some miracle the money might have come back in the meantime. He grew increasingly hot and flustered as he searched. And still he found nothing.

At last he had to face the dreadful conclusion. Olive must have taken it. She'd known where it was. She'd stolen it and walked out. Dan's sense of betrayal was overwhelming. He had befriended Olive and cared for her. She was the only friend he'd ever really had. And now this. It was almost the worst of the series of blows he'd suffered.

Dan was filled with sudden rage. He couldn't let her get away with this. He would go and catch her and make her give the money back. He knew she lived in the Shambles with a man called Frank and his brother Doug. The Shambles was a small area. He would surely be able to find her. Without giving himself time for second thoughts, he climbed down from his attic and headed determinedly along Canal Street.

The Shambles was at the other side of the canal company premises, beyond the railway sidings. The direct way was under the arches, but that required some complicated trespassing. It was quicker to go the long way round than to overcome all the obstacles.

From Canal Street you went up the lower part of

Camellia Hill, crossed the railway by the road bridge, and walked down Slaughter Street, a long narrow street lined with small shops and tumbledown houses. At the bottom of Slaughter Street you came to the wall that had surrounded the old slaughterhouse and its yards and pens. In the previous century, animals had been brought here by road or rail or canal-barge to be killed for food. Then the slaughterhouse had gone out of business and been demolished, and somebody had packed the site with small cheap dwellings for rent. They had been jammed together all higgledy-piggledy, making use of existing walls wherever they could.

The result was a warren of a place, built partly with bricks from the slaughterhouse itself. Wide-eyed children told horror stories of patches of blood, still sticky, or of ghostly screams heard from long-dead animals. That was all nonsense, of course, but the area was still called the Shambles and had a reputation for violence.

Set into the outer wall was an archway with a lamp above it, at present unlit. Through the archway you could glimpse a cobbled alley and crumbling soot-blackened buildings. If you went in there, you were in the inner citadel of slumdom.

Dan's spirits quailed as he stood outside the arch, but he pulled himself together, took a deep breath and marched in. The alley opened into another, which in turn opened into a third, and soon he was in a little maze of entries and passageways. In one of these lay a heap of stinking, uncovered garbage, and a couple of mongrel dogs were rooting in it, pausing occasionally to snarl at each other. Dan steered well clear of them.

Farther along the same alley was an outdoor tap, at which a fat, down-at-heel woman was filling a bucket. Dan asked if she knew a little lass called Olive. The woman looked vacantly at him and shook her head. Two other women gossiping on a doorstep broke off long

enough to tell Dan they'd never heard of any Olive.
Neither had an old man in cap and muffler who didn't lift
his eyes from the gutter while Dan was talking to him.

Two small girls squatting in the middle of a passageway and playing some kind of game with pebbles
were better informed.

'He must mean Frank's Olive,' said one to the other.

'That's right!' Dan said eagerly.

'I'll show you,' the child said. 'I'm not going too near,
though. Come on.' She led Dan farther into the maze.
Narrow dark entries ran in like veins among the brickwork. She pointed along one of them. 'Frank Ridgway's
is right at the end,' she said. 'The door that's open. Him
and Doug and Olive live there. Hey, what you want with
them?'

'Olive's a friend of mine, that's all,' said Dan.

'Oh. Well, if I was you I'd watch out. If Frank's in one
of his tempers, keep your distance. I'm off.' And the
child disappeared the way they'd come.

Dan walked warily up the entry, past two closed
doors. He listened at the open one, but couldn't hear any
voices. He tapped at the door, softly. No reply. He
knocked, first gently then loudly. Still no reply. Dan
pushed the door wider and, moving on tiptoe, stepped
cautiously inside.

The door opened into a small, bare and very dirty
room, with nothing in it except two wooden chairs, an
old deal table and a great many old newspapers. But the
room made no claim on Dan's attention; he hardly
noticed it. He was met and almost overwhelmed by
a sound and a smell coming from just beyond it: a sound
of sizzling and a rich, marvellous smell of cooking
meat.

Dan was drawn across the empty room as if under
hypnosis, and through a doorless opening into a tiny
kitchen. On a battered gas stove, a massive quantity of

steak and onions was being fried in a large pan. The cook was Olive.

Dan stared at her. She stared back at him. For half a minute neither of them said anything. The sizzling of the steak was loud in Dan's ears. Olive moved the frying-pan away from the flame. Her face was white, and there was the blotch of a new bruise on her right cheek.

'You took ...' he began; and then, pointing to the bruise, 'Who did that?'

She looked at him steadily but didn't answer.

'It was him, was it? Frank?'

Still no reply. She didn't even nod.

'You took my money, didn't you? And brought it to him?'

She shook her head and declared with passion, 'No, I never! They found it. I wouldn't tell them. That's why I got this.' In turn she pointed at the bruise.

'*Them*?' Dan said. '*They* found it?'

'Frank and Doug. They found where we was hiding. At least, Doug did. He'd seen us spending money in a shop, and followed us. Now, you get out of here, Dan, quick. Doug's in the house and Frank's coming back. Don't let them catch you!'

Dan stayed where he was.

'Go on!' she urged him. 'You seen what *I* got. It's nothing to what *you'll* get. Hop it!'

Dan said slowly. 'You spent my money on steak.'

'*They* did. Now, go. I'm telling you, go!' And then, with a note of despair, 'I *told* you! It's Doug!'

She was looking beyond him. Dan turned. Close behind him, Narrow-Eyes was standing.

'Hello, Daisy!' he said with a sour grin.

Dan stood open-mouthed. He was taken aback by the discovery that Narrow-Eyes was Frank's brother Doug. And he didn't like the look on the lad's face.

'I got you now, haven't I, Daisy?' Doug said; then, to Olive, 'You get on with cooking that steak! Frank'll be back any minute. It better be ready for him!' Turning back to Dan he went on, 'I know what you come for, Daisy. Well, you're getting something else instead. We got some unfinished business, remember?'

Narrow-Eyes gripped Dan by a wrist, twisted it painfully, and propelled him into the bare adjoining room. Then he faced Dan, grimaced, and spat in his eye. This was more than Dan could take. With the surge of strength that he'd felt on the previous occasion in the streets of the Jungle, Dan broke free and hit Narrow-Eyes hard in the face.

Narrow-Eyes aimed a kick at his groin. Dan dodged it, grabbed the foot in mid-air, and threw Narrow-Eyes on his back. Then he hurled himself on top and started banging the lad's head on the bare floorboards. Narrow-Eyes struck out blindly for Dan's face and landed a lucky blow that jolted his head back. Regaining the initiative, he pushed Dan away, struggled swiftly to his feet, and caught Dan again with a huge swinging blow to the stomach. Dan doubled up. Narrow-Eyes advanced upon him. And at that moment the door flew open, heavy feet thudded on the floorboards, and a massive body topped by a broad red beefy face loomed over the grappling pair.

'Frank! Gimme a hand!' gasped Narrow-Eyes.

Frank stepped between the two of them, tore them apart with his enormous paws, and sent them flying into opposite corners of the room.

'What the 'ell's all *this* about?' he demanded.

'He set on me!' Narrow-Eyes complained. 'In the Jungle last week. Bash him, Frank! Bash him!'

'Hold on a mo',' said Frank. His speech was slow; his brow was puckered with intellectual effort, 'He set on you? This kid set on you?' And then, with the air of one triumphantly producing the crucial question, 'What did he set on you for?'

'I didn't set on him,' said Dan sullenly.

'It's him that was in that attic with our Olive,' said Narrow-Eyes.

Frank complained to no one in particular, 'I come in hungry for me supper and find all this going on!' Then he turned to Dan and told him, 'You keep away from our Olive, see? If I catch you speaking to her again . . .' He clenched a fist, held it an inch from Dan's face, then drew it back and looked as if he was about to strike by way of demonstration.

Dan backed away, shuddering. Then he took a deep breath and said with nervous daring, 'W-w-what about my money?'

For a moment Frank looked uneasy. '*What* money?' he demanded.

'The money I hid in the attic.'

Narrow-Eyes chipped in. 'Hark at him!' he said. 'Telling us there was money in that old attic! *I* don't know nothing about no money, do you, Frank?'

'No,' said Frank; and then, giving the game away, 'Who says it was his money anyway? A lad his age wouldn't have that much money.' He turned to Dan. 'You musta nicked it.'

'I d-d-didn't!' Dan declared indignantly. 'I was given it. Jack Lunn gave it me. He's my mum's husband.'

'Jack Lunn, eh? I know Jack. He's an old pal of mine. Went off to Birmingham a few days ago, looking for work. He wanders, does Jack. Can't settle in one place.' Frank turned aside and yelled, 'Olive! When we going to get that steak? Hurry up or I'll come and remind you!' Then, addressing Dan again, 'Jack's a good pal. If he'd known I was skint, he'd have *wanted* me to have that money. Just the same as if Jack was skint and I had money I'd give it him. So that's that. You're not getting no money from me. Bugger off out of here and be thankful you're getting out in one piece!'

'Why don't you clout him, Frank?' asked Doug, disappointed.

'You clout him if you like. I want me supper.' Frank led the way into the other room. Doug, who didn't seem altogether keen to restart the fight without assistance, followed him, and so did Dan. Olive came in from the kitchen carrying two tin plates laden with steak and onions.

Frank sat down. On his way into the house he'd parked some bottles of beer on the kitchen table. He knocked the cap off one of them by striking it deftly against a corner of the table, then put the bottle to his mouth and took a deep swig. Olive brought two battered knives and forks. Narrow-Eyes looked sourly at Dan, but sat down opposite his brother, who was already gobbling steak at a great rate. After a minute Frank swallowed, took another swig of beer, and said to Dan, 'Well, go on, then. Hop it. There's nowt for you here.'

Dan stood his ground. He had another point to raise.

'D-d-don't hit Olive any more!' he said nervously.

'You *what*?' Frank shovelled more steak into his mouth and spoke through it. 'Olive'll get hit if she deserves it. If she don't deserve it, she won't get hit.'

'You might be in trouble with the police or the Cruelty Man if you kept on hitting her,' Dan said.

'Listen, you. This is the Shambles. Police don't come in here if they can help it. If they do come in, they come in pairs. As for the Cruelty Man, I'll cruelty *him* if he starts any nonsense with me!' Frank swallowed. 'And now, if I have to get up from this table it won't be the police you need *or* the Cruelty Man, it'll be the undertaker!'

'Go on, Dan,' said Olive quietly. 'You better go.'

Dan knew when he was beaten. He went. When he was halfway along the entry, Olive caught up with him.

'Come on!' he said. 'Let's run for it!'

'Don't be daft, Dan. Where would we run to? I got to stay; there's nothing else for it. Don't worry, they won't really hurt me. I don't mind a bruise or two. But you got off lightly, Dan, you did, honest. Frank's in a good temper, for him. If he'd been in one of his moods you'd have copped it. Anyway, thank you, Dan, for looking after me. I'm sorry about your money.'

'I'll see you again, won't I?' Dan asked.

'I dunno. Don't come *here* again. That's what I'm warning you about. You're asking for trouble, coming here. Now, I better get back or *I'll* be for it. Bye, Dan!'

'Bye,' said Dan. He walked out of the Shambles and set off up Slaughter Street. The smell of steak and onions lingered as a memory in his nostrils. It was getting towards dusk and he was faint with hunger. There was no food left in the attic, and he couldn't buy any now. He was totally down-and-out.

This surely was the end of his independence, a bitter end. There was no point any longer in consulting Uncle Bert. He would pick up his satchel, head for Aunt Verity's, and surrender.

CHAPTER 18

Walking down Camellia Hill on his way back to Canal Street, Dan had to pass Aunt Annie's Homely Dining-Room and Working Man's Restaurant, known as Annie's for short. It was drawn to his attention by an oblong patch of light thrown across the pavement and by a strong, savoury smell. At Annie's you could get a good meal for a shilling: soup, meat and two vegetables, and a heavy lump of pudding with custard. Tea was a penny a cup extra.

Dan went past Annie's, then halted and, as if drawn back irresistibly, retraced a few steps and pressed his nose against the window. Through a veil of steam he could see a row of tables, ranged along the far wall and divided by high-backed benches so as to give a degree of privacy to each. Each table had a stained white cloth on it, and a young girl was serving, in the intervals of chatting with customers. All but one of the tables were occupied, for Annie's gave good value and was popular.

Dan's stomach was rumbling with emptiness. What he needed most in the world at that moment was a good meal, but he didn't have a shilling. As he watched, a young man and his girl came out of the restaurant, accompanied by a blast of warm, rich, steamy air. Dan sighed deeply as it met his nostrils, and rummaged through his pockets, though he knew perfectly well there were only two or three coppers in them. He sighed again and reapplied his nose to the glass.

The young couple were walking away, but now the girl stopped and drew her companion to a halt.

'See that poor little lad?' she said. 'Just look at his face. I'n't it pathetic?'

Her friend said nothing and looked as if he wanted to move on, but the girl prevented him.

'Are you hungry?' she asked Dan.

Dan, embarrassed, nodded.

'When d'you last have a meal?'

'L-l-last night.'

'Did you hear that, Stan? He hasn't eaten since last night. Here, I got to do something about that. Just a minute, lad.'

She rummaged in her handbag. The young man pulled a leather purse from his pocket.

'Allow *me*!' he said with an expression of benevolence. 'Here y'are, lad, here's a shilling. Get yourself a meal!'

Dan had never taken money from a stranger in his life before. Grandpa and Mum had always told him not to, as a matter both of pride and prudence. He tried to stammer out a refusal, but it wouldn't come.

'There, that'll do him a bit of good,' the young man said. He looked as if he hoped it would do *him* a bit of good with his girl. She smiled up into his face and he tucked her arm under his. They walked away up the street, leaving Dan still looking at the shilling in his palm.

The feeling that he should give it back didn't last long. He went straight into Annie's and seated himself at the empty table. The young girl detached herself un-hurriedly from a talkative group at the next table and offered Dan a greasy menu-card. He chose steak and kidney pudding.

'Gimme the shilling first,' the girl said. 'We don't take no chances with young lads.'

Dan paid, and in due time received a bowl of piping-hot soup, followed by his main course. He bolted this greedily, but slowed down a good deal over the jam roly-poly which concluded the meal. As he spooned up the last of the custard, he became aware that somebody had seated himself at the other side of the table and was watching him with interest.

Somebody he knew. A tall, sturdy lad in mid-teens with villainously cropped hair, a strawberry birthmark on his cheek, and a quizzical expression. It was Leo.

'Hullo, Daisy,' he said.

Dan looked up warily and said nothing.

'How's things, Daisy?'

Another silence.

'There, aren't you talking to me tonight? I'm your pal, remember? I saved your life, more or less. Now, listen to me, Daisy. I said, "Hullo, how's things?"'

'All r-r-right,' said Dan.

'I've forgot your real name.'

'It's D-d-d-dan. Dan Lunn.'

'Awright, Dan. I'm Leo Rogers ... You still got that picture of your mum, Dan?'

Dan nodded.

'Let's have another look at it.'

Silently Dan passed it across the table. Leo studied it for a minute before handing it back. 'I like that face,' he said. 'There's something about it. She has class, your mum. I expect she looks after you just like she should.'

Dan didn't want to deny it. He was silent yet again.

'So why,' Leo demanded, leaning sharply across the table, 'was you begging outside here just now?'

'I wasn't b-b-begging,' said Dan indignantly. 'I didn't ask for anything. They g-g-gave me a shilling. It was their idea.'

The serving-girl came to their table. 'You want anything?' she said to Leo. 'This ain't free seating, you know. As for you, lad' – she looked at Dan – 'if you've finished, it's time you was on your way.'

'Bring us a cup of tea each,' said Leo grandly, producing two pennies. The girl went off and came back with strong, sweetened tea in thick white mugs.

'Seems to me, Dan,' said Leo thoughtfully, 'that you was real hungry a few minutes ago. I reckon that pretty mum of yours ain't supporting you. What's more, Dan, I got a hunch you're on your own!'

There was something about Leo that invited confidences. Suddenly Dan found himself telling of everything that had happened to him. Out it all came in an unstoppable flood. Leo listened gravely without interrupting. When Dan had finished, he inquired, 'What you going to do now, Dan?'

Dan admitted, shamefaced, that he was on the point of giving up and surrendering to Aunt Verity.

'It don't sound much fun, doing that,' Leo said. 'And I don't like the sound of that Basil. If you want *him* done over, just let me know. But listen, Dan. For one that wasn't begging, you did all right, didn't you? You hadn't been here a minute before somebody came up and gave you the price of a meal. You know something, Dan? You have a really appealing look. Sort of wide-eyed. A look like that has possibilities.'

'I d-d-don't know what you mean,' said Dan.

'Aye, well, you been sheltered till recently, haven't you, up there in the Daisies? Down here, you got to make use of whatever you have, even if it ain't much. I know the world, young Dan. I been around a lot longer than you have. You know how old I am?'

Dan shook his head.

'I'm sixteen, nearly seventeen,' said Leo impressively. 'Left school two years back. I know what's what. Now let me tell you a thing or two. First, about this mum of yours. You may not believe it just now, but it's long odds she'll come back before too long. They do, you know. They walk out because they've had a row or they fancy some feller, and then after a while they have another row or the new feller lets them down or they feel sorry for what they've done, and back they come. I can't *promise* you, Dan, but I reckon one of these days you'll be seeing her again.'

Leo's tone had been confident. Now it became knowing.

'But you don't want to go into Broad Street children's home, Dan. Don't have nothing to do with Broad Street. I could tell you a thing or two about that place.' Leo rolled his eyes. 'Up at six every morning. Queue up to wash in cold water that you have to break the ice on in winter. Scrub all the floors before breakfast. Then a little bowl of porridge, and if you don't swaller it quick the bigger lads grab it. Stand to attention for half an hour, waiting to be

112

inspected by the warden, and God help you if you make a sound. Then school, and they beat you if you get a sum wrong; beat you black and blue if you're not blue with cold already. Little bowl of stew for dinner, if you ain't been put on bread and water for something you didn't even know you'd done wrong. Bit of bread and marge for tea. Then peel the spuds for tomorrow's stew and scrub the floors again before you go to bed . . .'

'It's not *really* like that, is it?' said Dan, horrified.

''Course it is. A pal of mine's just come out of there. He says, in another fortnight they'd have had to carry him out in a box. A pauper's coffin. In fact,' said Leo with relish, 'lots of 'em *do* come out in a coffin. They *prefer* 'em to die, in Broad Street, 'cause it saves the cost of keeping 'em.'

'I don't believe it,' said Dan; but he wasn't quite sure.

'Well, now, you may be thinking that even your auntie's would be better than that. And you may be right, Dan, you may be right. *But* . . .' Leo paused for effect. 'There could be another way out for you. Another way of passing the time till your mum comes back, better than Broad Street *or* your auntie's. You're not in a hurry tonight, are you? Why don't you come home with *me*? Get to know my folks, like.'

'B-b-but why?'

''cause there might be a bed for you. Just for a night or two if you liked, while you sort things out. It don't do to act too hasty, Dan. There's always room in our place. Any pal of mine is welcome. And you're a pal, Dan.'

'Would your mum and dad *have* me?'

'Well, they ain't my mum and dad, strictly speaking. But they might as well be. We all call them Mam and Pop. They'd treat you well, Dan, I can promise you that.'

'Where do you live, Leo?'

'Bank House. In Bougainvillea Gardens.'

'Oh. You mean Buggy Street.'

'Some call it that,' Leo admitted.

Dan frowned. Everyone knew Bougainvillea Gardens, and everyone called it Buggy Street. It was a row of once-elegant three-storey houses right on the canal bank west of Hibiscus Street: formerly occupied by well-to-do business men but now decaying and mostly rented out room by room to an ever-changing population of hawkers, market traders, rag-and-bone men, bookmakers' runners, and casual workers of the roughest kind.

Buggy Street was of doubtful reputation, to say the least. Dan hesitated.

Leo grinned. It was a warm, wide, friendly grin.

'You do right to be careful,' he acknowledged. 'There's some funny 'uns in Buggy Street. But my lot are all right. We got a whole house there. I told you, it's called Bank House, that's its real name, always was. We're a family. Well, sort of.'

Dan still hesitated. Leo's grin was replaced by a hurt and puzzled frown. 'What you worrying about, Dan?' he asked. 'I looked after you all right before, didn't I? When Doug and that lot caught you, you was in a nasty situation, and I got you out of it. Why should you think I'd land you in any trouble now?'

'Well . . .' Dan began uncertainly. 'I mean . . . well, I don't know why you're interested.'

Leo now seemed to be offended.

'It's 'cause I *like* you, Danny. That's all there is to it. But if you don't trust me, you'd best not come. If there's no trust between pals, it's a poor lookout.' He pushed his mug away and half rose from his seat. 'You best go back to your auntie's and see if you get sent to Broad Street. If you do, I hope you come out alive, that's all.'

'I *do* trust you,' said Dan hastily. 'It's just . . . well, I haven't had time to think about it.'

'Give yourself time, then.' The friendly grin returned to Leo's face. 'Come and stay just for a night. You can go

114

on to your auntie's whenever you want. Tomorrow morning, if you like. Nobody's going to kidnap you. But it's my guess, when you find out what it's like at Bank House you'll want to stay.'

'Yes, well . . .'

'That's right, Danny. I knew you'd see sense. And you know what? I reckon it'll be a nice change for you to see a bit of family life. You've not had much of *that* lately, have you?'

Dan admitted that he hadn't.

'There you are, then. Bank House for you! Now, stop staring into the bottom of that mug and come along with Leo!'

Leo waved airily to the girl as they left. 'Bye, love!' he called. She didn't respond, but Dan was impressed by Leo's style.

'You're doing right,' Leo told him when they were out in the street. 'You stick with me and you got a great future!'

CHAPTER 19

Dan's steps were flagging as he accompanied Leo down to the bottom of Camellia Hill and through a tangle of Jungle streets to Bougainvillea Gardens. He'd had a hard day and walked long distances already. And he felt apprehensive, wondering if he'd agreed too readily to go with Leo. Perhaps he was on his way to some appalling den of vice and corruption . . .

Away from Camellia Hill there weren't any lights apart from those that shone from humble corner public-houses and late-opening shops. Shadowy figures lurched or flitted through streets and alleyways, giving the impression that the darkness had brought them out and they'd never appear by day. By some strange means, many of them recognized and were recognized by Leo. Once a gang of half a dozen lads approached, and Dan feared that he and Leo were going to be set on, but after a brief exchange of words the gang sheered off.

'They know me,' Leo explained. 'We're pals.' It seemed that everyone was Leo's pal.

A lamp shone over one of the front doors in Bougainvillea Gardens, and it was to this one that Leo led the way. It was a handsome door with a fanlight above. With a flourish Leo took a key from his pocket, opened it and ushered Dan inside. They crossed a hall and went down a couple of steps to a room which at first sight seemed full of people.

It was a warm, comfortable, slightly shabby room, and Dan's first reaction was to feel reassured. It certainly didn't look like a den of vice. A huge coal fire roared in an open grate. A small man, open-necked and shirt-sleeved with a narrow, humorous face was narrating some anecdote, loudly, and gesturing with his hands in illustration. A much younger man with black hair and a very white face sat at an upright piano in a corner, half-turned towards the speaker and strumming very softly with one hand. A couple of young women, one fair and one dark, sat side by side on a sofa, heads together, and a strikingly handsome brown-haired young man was in an armchair close by. Sprawling on the hearthrug was a boy somewhere around Dan's age, reading a comic. Dan noticed that there were bottles and glasses around and that the adults, including the two girls, were smoking cigarettes. Grandpa would not have approved of that. Otherwise it looked a respectable family gathering such as would have done credit to the Marigolds or even the Chrysanthemums.

116

Everyone looked round as Leo and Dan came in; two or three voices said 'Hello' and somebody moved a chair back so that they could sit side by side on the carpet. The small man went on with his story, which seemed complicated and continued for some time. Eventually he finished, among a scatter of laughs. Then he turned to Leo and said, 'Who's this?'

'It's Dan. A pal of mine. Needs a bed for the night.'

'Hello, Dan,' the small man said; and, to Leo, 'He's a little 'un, isn't he? How old is he? Ten?'

'I'm twelve!' Dan declared indignantly.

'Twelve, is he?' the small man said, still speaking to Leo. 'That's still young to be on his own. *Is* he on his own, Leo?'

'Yes.'

'Where's he been sleeping till now?'

'In that row of old cottages, down by the viaduct.'

'He's not a runaway, is he? With police and relatives after him?' Leo referred the question to Dan. 'Nobody's after you, are they, Danny?'

'No,' said Dan. 'My aunties think I'm with my mum, and my mum's gone. Nobody cares where I am.' There was a catch in his voice as he said this. Suddenly he was deeply sorry for himself.

'Poor little lad!' said the fair-haired girl.

'You're among friends now, Dan,' said Leo reassuringly.

Everyone in the room was now looking at Dan.

'I'll introduce you,' Leo said. 'Did you all hear, folks? This is my friend Dan. Dan, this is Pop you just been talking to. And this is Doris and Elsie.'

The two girls were probably both about twenty. Doris was buxom, blonde, blue-eyed, round-faced and wide-mouthed. She looked tough but friendly. 'Hello, Dan,' she said. Elsie was dark-haired, swarthy and withdrawn. She didn't say anything.

117

'And Joe,' Leo continued.

Joe, sitting on the piano stool, was thin, sharp-eyed and seedy-looking, as if he never went out of doors. He was probably seventeen or eighteen. He drew on a cigarette and scrutinized Dan through the smoke, unsmilingly.

''lo, kid,' he said, and struck a chord with his free hand.

'And Ray.'

With his sleeked-back hair and conscious good looks, Ray reminded Dan of the handsome heroes he'd seen flickering seductively across the screen during his rare visits to the Picture Palace, over in Claypits. Ray didn't say anything, but moved a hand in a gesture that was halfway to being a wave.

'And Titch.'

Titch was smaller than Dan, and at first sight looked younger. But he was probably at least as old. He had the ageless, shrewd and wary look of one who had never been a child. After a quick glance at Dan, he returned to his comic without a word.

'And, just coming in, this is Mam,' said Leo finally.

Mam was fat and shapeless. Her face was round, her colour high, and she had a broad smile, only slightly impaired by gap teeth. She wore a dirty apron and down-at-heel slippers.

'Hello, Leo,' she said. 'Hello, lad, whoever you are. Welcome to Buggy Street. I bet you're both hungry, aren't you?'

'I'm famished,' said Leo. 'Dan's had a meal, but I dare say he could eat another.'

'He does look thin,' said Mam in a tone of concern.

'There you are!' Leo said to Dan. 'That's the effect you have on them. They all want to feed you up!'

Mam took no notice of this remark. 'I got a big pot of

stew on the range next door,' she said. 'With dumplings. I'll bring you a bowl each.'

Dan declined a bowl of stew. The steak and kidney pudding and jam roly-poly were lying heavy on his stomach. He didn't feel hungry at all, but he was increasingly sleepy. He pulled himself together.

'Are you all one family?' he inquired.

'You could call us that,' said Pop. He winked, at no one in particular. 'One big happy family, that's us. What did you have in mind for this lad to do, Leo?'

'We'll leave it till tomorrow, Pop, shall we?' Leo said. 'Let him get used to us. He's too tired to think about anything tonight.'

Mam still seemed concerned over Dan's failure to eat.

'You *sure* you won't have no stew, lad?' she asked. 'What about another helping for you, Leo?'

Leo ate more stew. Except for the two girls, who chatted together on the sofa, and Titch, who finished his comic and began another, everyone then started playing a card game on the carpet. It was a very simple game, in which the player who drew the highest card from the pack was the winner. Everyone put stakes on it: not just pennies but sixpences and shillings. At one point, Pop staked a whole half-crown on the turn of a card and lost it without a murmur. He, Ray and Joe drank beer from bottles. The fug in the warm room grew. Dan nodded. Somebody put him in an armchair, where he curled up and dozed. He woke to find the gathering breaking up.

'Time we was off, Joe lad,' Pop was saying. 'We got to meet Parker, the other side of town.'

'You're g-g-going out, Mr . . . er . . . Pop?' asked Dan.

'Yes. Joe and me's going out. Out on business.' Pop winked again at nobody in particular. 'We got an important call to make.'

'Take care,' said Mam. 'Don't do nothing silly.' She kissed them both.

The two girls had disappeared from the room while Dan was dozing, and he hadn't noticed. Now they came briefly back into it. They were dressed in little smart jackets and short skirts, and were wearing heavy make-up.

'Bye, Mam,' said Doris.

'Bye, love,' said Mam. More kisses were exchanged. Doris left a large lipstick mark on Mam's cheek, which she didn't notice.

'*They* can't be going out to business as well?' Dan said.

Ray and Leo both laughed. Mam looked a little embarrassed. Titch screwed the second comic into a ball and said, ' '*Course* they're going to work. What do you think they are?'

But Dan didn't understand.

'It's the funniest family I ever saw,' he said; and gave a huge yawn.

'Time you went to bed, Danny,' said Mam. 'He can kip down with you, can't he, Titch?'

'No, he can't,' said Titch sourly. 'There ain't no room in my place. I'm not moving all my stuff out for *him*.'

'Now that's not nice, Titch, it isn't really!' Mam protested. 'You should *welcome* Dan. But seeing he may not be staying, I s'pose he can sleep on the sofa tonight.'

Dan was three-quarters asleep already. He could half hear the others talking over him, though he didn't really take it in.

'I don't think you should have brought him here, Leo,' Mam was saying. 'He's too innocent. He don't belong with us at all.'

'He has an auntie up in the Chrysanthemums,' said Leo. 'Maybe I should take him back to her. But just look at his face. Worth a fortune, that face is.'

'Poor little soul,' said Mam. 'I wouldn't like him to come to no harm. I've fair taken to him.'

'You see?' said Leo triumphantly. 'He's a walking

gold-mine, if we handle him right. And he won't come to any harm. He'll be better off than he's ever been in his life, if he comes in with us!'

'You can talk to Pop about it in the morning,' Mam said. 'I shall wait up for Pop, myself. I always worry about him when he's out on business. But, just for now, I'm going to make this lad comfortable.'

Dan was vaguely aware of being stretched out on the sofa, having a blanket spread over him, and hearing the fire being stoked up.

'Goodnight, Danny Boy,' said Mam.

She bent over and kissed him. It was the first time he'd been kissed goodnight since his own mother left. The feel of the kiss on his cheek stayed with him as he sank into the depths of sleep.

CHAPTER 20

Dan was awakened by a clatter of pans in a nearby room. It was daylight. For a moment he couldn't remember where he was. Then it came back to him. He'd been put to bed on a sofa in Buggy Street. The room he was in was empty of people now, but had an unpleasant smell of stale cigarette-smoke. He got off the sofa and made his way hesitantly across the hallway into a large, square kitchen with a red quarry-tiled floor and a big open range. In the middle of it was a large, scrubbed deal table. As he looked around, Mam emerged from a scullery at the far end, drying soapy hands.

'Dan, love!' she said cheerfully. 'How are you? Slept well?'

Dan nodded.

'Pop and Leo's around. The rest of 'em's still in bed. They're not early risers. Now, let me make you some breakfast. Do you like bacon?'

Dan nodded. The steak and kidney pudding was a memory now, and he felt hungry again. Mam put bacon into a pan which soon sizzled on the big black range. Dan ate by himself at the big deal table and drank hot sweet tea while Mam finished whatever she was doing in the scullery. She came back and said, 'The lav's in the yard. And you could do to wash your face, Danny Boy. I can't see what it's like under all that grime.'

Dan hadn't washed his face for days. It hadn't seemed a very urgent task. Mam brought hot water in an enamel bowl, and a bar of soap.

'Here, let me do it,' she said. When she'd finished, she rubbed him dry with a bit of rough towel. Then she took a good look at him.

'There, you're a nice-looking lad,' she said. 'I can see why Leo thinks you've got a future.'

'W-w-what sort of future?' Dan asked.

'Nay, he'll have to tell you himself, him and Pop. I don't touch the business side of things, not usually. I got enough to do, looking after 'em all. Now, why don't you tell Mam all about it, and how you came to be on your own?'

Dan began to tell his story again, but when he came to his desertion by his mother he found a lump coming in his throat. Mam saw his distress and clasped him to her bosom.

'There, there,' she said. 'Maybe she'll come back. If she don't come back, she's no good and you're well rid of her. So it's no use worrying, is it? But have a good cry if it helps.'

Dan might have done so if there'd been any privacy. But as Mam spoke, Ray came into the kitchen. He sat down opposite Dan and listened with interest to the latter part of his story. Dan kept glancing at him. Ray was wearing a well-pressed suit and a dazzling tie, and his brushed-back hair was glossier than ever. But there was something different about Ray this morning.

'You're wearing a moustache!' Dan said.

'That's right,' said Ray cheerfully.

'He does wear one from time to time,' said Mam in a conversational tone.

'Makes a quick change,' said Ray. 'When folk describe you, a moustache is the first thing they think of, see? So I have one I can take off. Suits me, doesn't it? Makes me look like an ex-officer. There's plenty of those around in my line of business.'

'He's in motorcars,' Mam explained.

'B-b-but why do you need . . . ?'

'You'll find out,' said Ray. 'Hello, Titch. You look as if you'd found a penny and lost sixpence.'

Titch had mooched into the kitchen. He looked at Dan with distaste and sniffed the air.

'Somebody's been having bacon!' he said.

'Yes,' said Mam. 'Danny. I made it for him.'

'What about me?'

'You can have some if you want. It's in the pantry. You know how to fry bacon.'

Titch scowled.

'I did it for Dan 'cause he's new here,' Mam said. 'He might not be staying anyway. He's a guest, you might say.'

Titch scowled again.

'I don't want no bacon,' he said.

'I knew you didn't. You don't like me doing it for someone else, that's all.'

'I'll just have a slice of bread.' Titch cut himself a ragged slice from the loaf of bread on the table and buttered it heavily.

'We don't need no fancy-boys here,' he said.

'Titch,' said Ray, 'you're a pain in the backside. Belt up, will you? Now, Danny, if you're ready, Pop and Leo'd like to see you in the office.'

'The *office*?'

'That's a joke, sort of. There's a room at the top of the house where Pop keeps things that come to him in the way of business. Leo put a notice on the door once, saying OFFICE, and it's stuck. 'Course, it's not like a company office, with clerks and typewriters and such. But we're organized here. Go straight up the back stairs, Danny, and you'll find them both waiting for you. I have to go out and do a deal. See you later. So long.'

Dan made his way up two flights of stairs and then a narrow winding stairway, at the top of which was a small attic room. Pop was sitting at a trestle-table with papers scattered over it; Leo leaned against the window. Around the sides of the room, items of what looked like junk lay in heaps: silver, brass and copper ware, clocks and watches, assorted ornaments, necklaces and bracelets, photograph frames, inkstands, trays, hairbrushes and much else.

Leo beckoned to Dan to join him at the window. It looked out directly over the canal. From it you could see two or three bridges, the railway viaduct and acres of squat dirty houses, with the high buildings of the city centre just visible in the distance. Pop, seated at the table, tilted his chair back, tucked his thumbs into his armpits, and surveyed Dan benevolently.

'Well, young feller, how are we today?' he asked.

'All r-r-right, thank you,' Dan said.

'Now, what you want to do? Leo told me all about you. Like he said, you can go straight back to your auntie if you want. Nobody's stopping you. But I can see from your face you're not too keen on the idea.'

He paused. Dan said nothing.

'Well, now,' Pop went on, 'there's another possibility.

We quite like the look of you, Danny. Seems to me that *you* could do with a family and *we* could do with a smart lad like you. Why don't you join *our* family?'

Dan stared at him, bewildered.

'You could give it a try, couldn't you?' Pop went on. 'A trial on both sides, eh? See how we get on together.'

'B-but ...'

'You don't understand, do you, Danny?' said Leo tolerantly. 'You haven't come across a family like ours before. I better try to explain. You see, we're not related to each other, strictly speaking. In fact we've come together by accident. One person meets another, like I happened to meet you, and brings them home. Then, if we all get on with them...'

'And if they have something to contribute ...' Pop added.

'We might ask them to join us,' Leo concluded.

'W-w-what *sort* of thing do they have to contribute?' Dan asked.

'Well, we all got our talents, Danny,' said Pop. 'I'll explain to you in a minute. But there's one thing you better realize from the start. Most of what we do ain't strictly legal. In fact some of it ain't at all legal. Now, don't look so worried, lad. That don't mean we're a bunch of crooks.'

Pop tilted his chair farther back. He seemed to enjoy holding forth.

'You see, Danny,' he went on, 'this is a hard world. It's an unjust world. There's some that lives in big houses with dozens of servants and never wanted for anything all their lives. And there's some that's got nothing; some that's poor and starving. Millions, in fact.

'Are you follering me, Dan?' Pop was getting warmed up. 'Now there's some of us that has a conscience about this, some of us that wants to see it put right. And we don't think it'll be put right by folks marching up and

125

down with banners. Oh, no. If you want to put something right, you go out and do it yourself. And that's what we do. Scholars and suchlike call it the redistribution of wealth.'

'In short,' said Leo, 'nicking stuff.'

'Now, now, Leo,' said Pop. 'That's putting it crudely. Don't give Danny the wrong idea. It's true that sometimes we come into possession of what might be called other folk's property. In fact some of our associates practise the art of what the layman might think of as burglary; and incidentally, Danny, let me tell you that burglary is a risky and highly skilled occupation, to be looked on with respect. But we don't do no burglaries ourselves. We merely provide financial services for some of those what do. We help them turn their gains into cash. And we only deal with those that practise their art in well-to-do parts like Highwood or Overley. We wouldn't have anything to do with robbing the poor.'

'The poor haven't anything worth taking,' said Leo.

'That's not the point,' said Pop severely. 'The word I want to emphasize to young Danny is "redistribution". Mind you, Danny, what I've just told you about is only a corner of our practice. Some of us have quite different skills. Ray, for instance. He's a trader in motorcars. That's an up-and-coming business. We always try to look ahead, and we reckon the motorcar has a future. So Ray buys and sells them.'

'Buys them with dud cheques and sells them quick for cash,' said Leo.

'Anyone'd think you were trying to put our young friend off,' complained Pop.

'I just want him to know what he's in for,' said Leo. 'Fair's fair.'

'You make it sound *sordid*, Leo. The fact is, these people who own or want to own motors are the well-to-do. The day may come when the common man will own his own motorcar, but it hasn't arrived yet. Ray – er – *out-manoeuvres* people who can afford to lose a little.'

'But it's cheating, isn't it?' said Dan, shocked.

'Some might call it that. But it'd be truer to say that Ray performs a service for these people. He teaches them a lesson they won't forget, namely, not to take cheques from strangers. They won't do it again after they once done it with Ray. If the truth was known, I dare say some of 'em's thankful to Ray for teaching them that lesson.'

'He don't wait to be thanked, though,' said Leo.

'Then there's Joe,' said Pop. 'He teaches a similar lesson, just as valuable. He teaches folk not to play cards with people they don't know. If they play cards with Joe, they lose. He's a first-rate billiards player, too, though that don't offer quite the same scope for making the luck run your way. And with him being a pianist as well, they like Joe in the clubs. Clubs are his natural habitat, so to speak.'

Dan's eyes had grown wider and wider.

'What does Titch do?' he inquired.

'Titch is a smart lad. He's what the layman would call a pickpocket. That's another means of redistribution, Danny Boy. Titch parts people from wealth what they don't need and gives it to them that do.'

'Namely, us,' said Leo.

'He's an artist, young as he is,' said Pop reverently. 'Like Joe, he has skill in his fingers. With his abilities, he could be a surgeon or anything he fancied. He could steal your underpants, Titch could, and you wouldn't know they'd gone. Where there's a race meeting or a fair or a football match – anywhere where there's lots of people with their minds on other things – there's Titch. And a rare nose he has for smelling out the right person and knowing just where he'll keep his wallet. There's some folk you might call buttoned-up: they keep their money in an inside pocket or a purse or something, and their hand on it all the time. Titch don't waste his efforts on *them*. A nice cheerful feller that's free and easy with his money and shoves it in his back pocket careless-like, that's the kind Titch likes.'

'Mind you,' said Leo, 'I reckon Titch is getting too big for his boots these days. Two years on the same lark and never been caught. He thinks he's the greatest.'

'*And* he's spoiled,' said Pop thoughtfully.

'That's with being the baby of the family. Mam and the girls always made a fuss of him. But if *Dan* was to join us' – Leo grinned knowingly at Pop – 'Titch wouldn't be the youngest any more. And Titch don't get no sweeter with time. Dan's twice as appealing as what Titch is.'

'That, Leo,' said Pop, 'is a very good point. It wouldn't do Titch no harm to get his nose put out of joint a bit.'

Dan didn't much like the sound of Titch or his activities. He hadn't altogether liked the way Titch looked at him, either.

'And the girls?' he inquired. 'What do *they* do?'

'Well,' said Pop. He sounded a little embarrassed. 'The girls is in what you might call the love business.'

'The *love* business?'

'Yes. You see, Danny, there's some fellers that don't have no nice wife or lady friend to love them. And they miss it, naturally. Well, Doris and Elsie are good-natured girls, see. They don't mind keeping a feller company.'

A blush spread slowly across Dan's face.

'I see you understand me,' said Pop. 'P'raps it's just as well that you do. But don't let me hear you making no unseemly comments. You treat Doris and Elsie with respect. They're young ladies in the love business, and that'll do for you. And now, Danny Boy, why don't you go with Leo and let him explain what we have in mind for *you*?'

'Danny has a nice-looking mum,' said Leo. 'He's got a

real classy photo of her. She looks a proper lady. Show Pop the picture, Danny.'

Dan felt in his pocket for the photograph, then gasped in dismay.

'It's not there,' he said. 'And I know I had it when I got here last night.'

Pop and Leo looked at each other. Both grinned. Pop went from the room to the head of the stairs.

'Titch!' he called. 'Titch! Come here! I want you! And bring that photograph!'

CHAPTER 21

'Now, come on, Dan,' said Leo when the photograph had been recovered and Titch had been sent off scowling, 'you and me's going to have a good talk.'

The back of Bank House overlooked the canal. There was a rickety landing-stage to which an old flat-bottomed boat was tied up. Leo led Dan out on to the landing-stage and they sat at the end of it, dangling their feet. Rubbish and ancient timbers floated on the canal's surface. Almost opposite them was the skeleton of a half-sunk barge. Hazy sunlight fell on the black water. There was a faint unwholesome smell.

'You seen our family, Dan,' said Leo. 'You know about them now. They ain't a bad lot on the whole. What about giving it a try?'

'T-t-tell me what you want *me* to do,' Dan said.

'You can guess, can't you? Remember I was telling you last night you have an appealing look. Well, that's worth money. Hard cash. You ever seen folk begging in this city, Dan?'

'Yes,' said Dan, remembering with a shudder the beggars he'd seen in the streets from time to time. They were usually shuffling old men. Mum had been known to give a beggar a penny, and Uncle Bert when in a generous mood to give sixpence, but Grandpa would never have anything to do with beggars. If you gave them anything, he said, they'd only spend it on drink.

'Now there's only one kind of beggar that does well,' said Leo. 'Well enough, I mean, to make a serious profession of it; and that's children. Folk that wouldn't stump up a shilling to keep their poor old mother out of the workhouse will give to a child, so long as it's thin and pale and has the right expression. Well, you got the right expression, Dan. It's a heaven-sent gift, you might say. When I first saw you outside Annie's, the look on your face would have melted a heart of stone. If we just find you the right pitch, the cash'll come rolling in.'

Dan didn't like the sound of it.

'I've never begged,' he said. 'My grandpa would have died of shame to see me begging.'

Leo shook his head sadly.

'You're going to have to change your ideas, Danny,' he said. 'Or else go back to the Daisies.'

'But listen,' Dan said, 'the things you're doing are against the law, aren't they? I mean, burgling and cheating's *crime*. It's *wrong*.'

'Oh, Danny, Danny. You got so much to learn. Crime's what *other* folk call it. Police and magistrates and fancy folk up at Highwood, *they* call it crime. To us, it's just making a living. We do it the best way we can, same as anyone else.'

But Dan's Chapel upbringing wouldn't let him swallow that.

'It *is* wrong,' he said. ''*Course* it's wrong, dealing in stolen goods and swindling and thieving. Taking what don't belong to you.'

And, with memories of Chapel sermons, there came back to him suddenly the recollection of another of the storybooks read in Grandpa's parlour. Looking into the black canal water, he brought it to mind. It was the story of a boy named Willie, who had befriended a burglar and talked earnestly to him, night after night, persuading him of the error of his ways. And in the end the burglar had repented. He had given up his life of crime and obtained honest work, delivering coal. From his scanty wages he had struggled to compensate those he had robbed.

Many years later, when Willie was a grown man, he had re-encountered the former burglar, elderly now and a regular chapel-goer. The man had fallen on his knees in front of Willie – there was a picture of the grown-up Willie, tall, handsome and commanding, with the honest toiler in rough working clothes grovelling at his feet – and had thanked him amid floods of tears for saving him from a life of wickedness. And, the storyteller concluded, Willie knew that this poor man now walked in the ways of grace, his salvation assured. What was more, Willie knew that in due course he himself would receive a heavenly reward.

It was an inspiring story. Dan had a vision of himself, convincing the crime family of the wrongness of their ways. It might take time, but surely in the end he would prevail. He couldn't believe that Pop and Mam and Leo were not good people at heart, like Willie's burglar. He wasn't so sure about some of the others, but they would be a challenge . . .

'Anyway, *begging* ain't theft,' Leo was saying. 'Nobody *has* to give you anything. Begging's honest enough.'

'You can get into trouble for it,' Dan pointed out.

'That's true enough. It's the biggest danger. You got to watch out. If you spot a copper out of the corner of your

131

eye, slip away if you can before he sees you. But never start a pursuit. If there ain't time to get away, walk towards and past him as bold as brass. Nine times out of ten he won't be sure, and he won't pick you up.'

'You seem to know a lot about it,' said Dan.

'You bet I do. I was on the begging lark myself when I was smaller. I'm too big and ugly now. Nobody'd give me a cent. But I know all about it. With me to help, you'll get a good pitch and make money. You got a great chance, Danny Boy.'

Suddenly Dan's horizon looked brighter. Here were food and warmth and company on offer to him. He needn't do anything that was positively wrong. Meanwhile, he would work at reforming his hosts. If he didn't succeed, he would at least have tried.

A gleam of sunlight coaxed rainbow colours from an oily patch on the surface of the canal.

'All right, Leo,' Dan said. 'Why don't I give it a try? But I won't do any stealing or such.'

''Course you won't,' said Leo. 'Nobody at Bank House has to do anything they don't want. Do what you like, that's our motto. Shake on it, Danny Boy.'

They shook hands.

'Welcome, brother!' said Leo.

CHAPTER 22

The Bank House family adopted Dan without much fuss. In less than a week everyone was taking him for granted except Titch, who plainly resented the loss of his favoured place as the youngest member. Titch refused point-blank to share sleeping accommodation, and Dan

slept on the sitting-room sofa. It suited him very well. In
Buggy Street he was more comfortable than he'd ever
been in his life. There was warmth, company, ample
food and a total absence of rules. There was money, too.
Money flowed into the household and flowed out again.
There was money to go to the Picture Palace over in
Claypits, or to lose in the machines in the amusement
arcade, or to buy sweets and fizzy drinks.

Dan had some moral problems, however. He wasn't
entirely sure that his reforming intentions entitled him to
live on the proceeds of crime. In other ways, too, he
found the conduct of his new family shocking. The
language used by everyone, including the two girls, was
such as Grandpa could scarcely have believed in, let
alone tolerated. A great deal of smoking and drinking
went on; bets were placed with bookmakers and cards
were played for money. Dan refused virtuously to join in
any such activity.

Within a few days his scruples became generally
known and were regarded with amused tolerance.
Members of the family moderated their language when
he was around, though it still seemed to him to be pretty
lurid. Sources of income were not referred to in his
presence. When Ray came home with a thick wad of
notes, proceeds of the sale of a motorcar, everyone
insisted to Dan that the money was profit on an honest
deal. Dan, reassured, accepted a pound note as
pocket-money. When living with Mum he had received a
penny a week.

On Dan's second Sunday night at Bank House, there
was a singsong. Joe sat at the piano and, cigarette droop-
ing from lips, played popular song-tunes with great
verve and inaccuracy. Dan joined in singing the ones he
knew.

Mam said thoughtfully, 'Sounds to me like you've
quite a nice voice, Danny.'

'I used to sing in the Chapel choir,' Dan told them.

'Sing us a hymn, then!' said Mam. 'I always did like a nice hymn.'

Everyone agreed except Titch, who left the room in disgust. Dan saw an opportunity to open his campaign. His stammer never troubled him when singing. He began with 'Rock of Ages' and went on to 'Fight the Good Fight' and 'Abide with Me'. Joe picked up the tunes and put in a few flourishes of his own. The others listened appreciatively. Dan sang half a dozen more hymns. He felt inspired and inspiring. When he paused for a rest and a drink of pop, there was applause from everyone, including Joe at the piano.

'Oh, Danny Boy,' said Doris. 'You do summat to me, you do really. You make me feel I could live a better life!'

Dan didn't realize that she was being facetious.

'That's what I w-w-want to do,' he said, and blushed crimson.

'Just one more hymn,' Doris said, 'and I'd probably Turn to the Light.'

'All right,' said Dan obligingly. 'I'll sing "Jesus wants me for a Sunbeam".' Then he realized that Joe was almost falling off the piano stool with suppressed laughter. He looked round the faces in the room. Yes, they were all laughing. Dan reddened again and, humiliated, ran from the room. Mam followed him into the kitchen and folded him in her arms.

'There, there, Danny,' she said. 'They don't mean no harm. They like you really. Everybody likes you. It's just that . . . well, it's so *funny*!' She was trying not to laugh herself.

Dan perceived that the reform of the Bank House family was likely to be a long and uphill task. But he resolved to persevere with it.

For two or three weeks nothing more was said about begging. Dan began to hope it had been forgotten. But he was deceiving himself.

'Well, Danny Boy,' said Pop one morning. 'Time you started earning a living. I was bringing money home long before I was your age.'

'Times has changed,' said Mam. 'You don't expect 'em to start so early these days.'

'Dan has a lot to learn,' said Pop. 'Sooner he starts the better. And with begging, you got to learn on the job. You develop your own techniques, like, and learn to judge character. But I don't believe in starting on a poor pitch. We'll start *you* at the Royal Britannia Hotel, Danny.'

'There's real money there,' agreed Leo, coming into the room, 'if the nobs like the look of you. And they'll like the look of Danny all right. But . . . his clothes won't do.'

'I'll see to that tomorrow,' said Mam. And next day she came home with an armful of rags and tatters, bought for threepence the lot from a barrow. Dan's own clothes were the worse for wear by now, but they weren't in anything like such a state as these.

'It's only for work,' Mam assured him. 'You can change back when you get home.' She chopped off a pair of threadbare trousers at the knee, and opened up a seam at the back for his shirt to show through. The shirt itself was ripped apart at the shoulder. But Mam stitched stout pockets into his rags, to make sure that any money he was given was safe. 'You'll have to get used to going barefoot, too,' she told him. 'Watch where you step, specially while your feet's still soft.'

At six in the evening he was presented for inspection by Pop and Leo. There was some discussion over whether his face should be dirtied. Pop thought it should, but Leo disagreed.

'You're out of touch with public taste, Pop,' he said. 'I

been on the begging lark myself. People like 'em to be barefoot and ragged-arsed but clean and decent. They don't like unhygienic-looking beggars.'

The Royal Britannia Hotel was in the city centre. Dan had heard of it but never been there. Soft light and warmed air flowed out from its richly carpeted lobby.

'We got to talk to the doorman first,' Pop explained. 'You can't do nothing without he lets you. But it'll be all right. He knows me. We done business before.'

The doorman wore a magnificent navy-blue uniform with gold trimmings. He looked like an admiral at least. And he did indeed know Pop. In intervals between striding out on to the pavement, whistling for taxis and opening doors for well-dressed ladies and gentlemen to get in or out, he was willing to discuss Dan's début.

'All right,' he said eventually. 'Usual terms.' He cast an experienced eye on Dan. 'He looks scared stiff. But that won't do no harm. Should do well, this one should. Right size, right build, right expression, and well got up for the job.'

He turned and spoke to Dan himself. 'Now then, young feller-me-lad. You stay out in the street, see? No coming into my lobby. If you come inside I only have to chase you out, and it lowers the tone of the place. I may have to chase you off anyway, if somebody complains. If I do that, you wait ten minutes before you come back, see?

'Now, your best place to stand is just beside the door there, on the city side, where I can't see you. There's a bit of light from that lamp that'll show you off a treat, make you look all hollow-eyed. You don't have anything to do with folk that comes or goes by taxi; they're mine. Those that arrive or leave on foot are yours, and so are passersby. You can step out into their path, but if they don't stop, you step back again. Don't obstruct them; them that won't stop are the ones that's most likely to complain about you.'

'And you ask 'em for tuppence,' said Pop. 'No more, no less.' He said, in a parody of a childish whine, '"Gimme tuppence, mister, for a bit o' bread." Remember the bread, Danny. It's a rule of successful begging; always say what you want the money for. And there's nothing like bread to make folk think you're starving.'

'You finish at midnight prompt,' said the doorman. 'That's when I go off duty. Then you come round to my cubbyhole, just inside the staff entrance, and you tip your pockets out. I take a third of what you get, and you needn't try to diddle me. I'm up to all the tricks. One or two lads in the past have tried scarpering with the loot before I go off duty. They know I can't chase 'em. But it's not worth the candle, my boy. Do that just once and you'll never beg at any hotel in this city again.'

'That's right, Danny,' said Pop. 'Honesty is the best policy.'

CHAPTER 23

Dan took up his station at the city side of the main entrance. He was on his own now. Though it was still summer, the evenings were beginning to get chilly. He shivered in his rags, either with cold or nervousness, and it was some minutes before he could bring himself to approach anyone.

People passed the hotel continually. Many were with companions or intent on their own affairs, and didn't even notice Dan. Of those who saw him, most seemed to be embarrassed and changed course in order to steer clear. The first money he received was a shilling, thrown at rather than to him, by a fairly well-dressed middle-aged man who didn't smile or show any interest whatever but merely flung the coin and strode on.

Dan's special clients however were the people entering or leaving the Royal Britannia Hotel. These were invariably prosperous-looking. When twenty minutes had passed with no unsolicited gifts except the first shilling, he braced himself to accost a florid, kindly-looking gentleman accompanied by a fur-coated lady. And then he couldn't get the words out.

'G-g-gimme t-t-t-t . . .' he began, and was unable to finish the sentence. The gentleman studied him with concern.

'Deaf and dumb, I should think, my dear,' he remarked. 'Or possibly deficient.' He addressed Dan in a loud voice: 'Can you hear me, boy? Do you understand what I'm saying?'

Dan was alarmed. 'Y-y-y-yes,' he gasped.

'Oh, come along, George, he's just a beggar-boy,' the lady said.

The gentleman drew a coin from his pocket and pressed it into Dan's hand. 'Good luck, lad,' he said, and hurried after his wife. Dan thought from the feel of it that the coin was a penny, but when he looked he saw that it was half a crown.

As the evening wore on, he learned that guests coming out of the Royal Britannia, well fed and comfortable, were better prospects than those going into it intent on their meal. He began to distinguish between generous faces and mean ones, and his success rate improved steadily. By mid-evening he had taken enough money to be able to feel the weight of it in his pockets. Later the increasing cold showed up in his pinched face, and although the numbers both of hotel customers and passers-by diminished, a bigger proportion gave to him. But he grew more and more weary and miserable. Time, measured by the big clock outside the building society across the way, passed ever more slowly. After half past ten it hardly seemed to pass at all.

Dan had a fright when a couple of policemen came along. He saw them in good time and bolted down a side-street, reappearing with heart pounding a quarter of an hour later. All was clear; the policemen had gone on their way. At midnight, with the hotel lobby empty of people, the doorman beckoned to Dan and sent him round to the side entrance. Just inside was a tiny office, hardly more than a cupboard. The man came inside and closed the door.

'Tip your pockets out, lad,' he said.

Dan emptied his pockets on to a bare wooden table. There was quite a pile of silver and copper.

'Is that the lot?' the man asked.

Dan nodded. The doorman cast an expert eye over him, but there was nowhere on Dan's thin and ragged person where any more money could have been concealed.

'All right,' he said. He counted the money out. 'Two pounds, one and sixpence,' he announced. 'My share's fifteen bob.' He selected coins from the heap, taking the shillings and florins and the half-crown given by the kindly gentleman. Dan was left with the small silver and all the copper. He shovelled it back into his pockets.

'You ain't done so bad for a beginner,' the doorman said. 'I liked the way you scarpered when them coppers came along. Just you keep at it and you'll do well. Now, on your way. Don't hang about.'

Dan had gone only a few yards along the street when a motorcar drew up beside him. Ray was driving, Pop sat with him in the front, and Leo was in the back. They hailed Dan enthusiastically. Five minutes later he was sitting on the sofa in Buggy Street in front of a blazing coal fire, and Mam was putting a big bowl of steaming soup into his hands.

'Well, you done your first night's work, Danny Boy!' said Pop. 'How much did you make?'

Dan told them. They were impressed.

'What did I tell you?' said Leo, pleased with himself. 'Danny has the gift.'

They counted out his share and decided he had been swindled by the doorman but that there was nothing to be done. 'He's in the position of power, see,' said Pop. 'Them that has power often abuses it.'

'I c-c-couldn't do it again,' Dan said. 'Honest, I just couldn't.'

'Oh, you'll get used to it,' Pop assured him. 'Most folk feel like that when they're just starting work. It's only natural. Anyway, you needn't do it again for a day or two. Friday and Saturday it's Burdock Park races. We always make that a day out.'

There was the slam of a door, and Doris came in. She looked tired. She got a bottle out of the cupboard and poured herself what Dan now recognized as a large gin.

'You're home early,' Mam said to her. 'What's the matter? Too cold for customers?'

'I got a headache, that's all,' said Doris. 'Hullo, Danny Boy. You joined the world's workers, eh? Be thankful you're a lad. It ain't no fun on *our* lark, I can tell you.'

'I reckon,' said Leo thoughtfully, 'that young Danny'd do best on the pub singing.'

'There isn't the money in it,' Pop objected.

'Maybe not, but the Royal Britannia's too long a turn for Danny. Them doormen won't let you go before midnight, in case they miss their share. Now the pubs, you got to stay outside, admittedly, but you can leave soon after closing-time.'

'And get two or three shillings if you're lucky. And a kick in the pants if you're not.'

'Danny'll do better than that,' Leo said. 'He has the expression *and* the voice. Singing outside the right pub, he'll fill his cap with cash in no time.'

'Maybe,' said Pop doubtfully. 'Anyway, just for now, he needs to get his beauty sleep. Drink up, Doris, and get out.'

'He won't always want girls out of his room,' said Doris, and giggled.

'Shut up, you!' said Mam, shocked. 'Danny's a nice little lad. Don't you go corrupting him!'

But Dan hadn't heard this exchange. He was fast asleep.

CHAPTER 24

Dan didn't get to the races at Burdock Park. The day after his night's begging, he developed a feverish cold, and he spent the two days of the race meeting on the sofa in front of the fire. Mam, who wasn't interested in the races, plied him with hot drinks and a succession of dainties, and brought him an armful of comics from Mould's, the newsagents in Camellia Hill.

In spite of all this care, Dan found that illness made him miss his own mother more than ever. It also reminded him how he himself had looked after Olive. He wondered how she was, and resolved that when he was better he would try to find out. But he realized that since arriving in Buggy Street he had never in fact been out alone. There was always someone at his side.

For the rest of the Bank House family, the races were a

great event. The older members went off together and came home rather drunk on the first night and very drunk on the second. Pop was pleased with himself, having backed several winners. Titch had made much more money than Pop without any recourse to the bookmakers: a race meeting was his happiest hunting ground, and he'd relieved a number of careless racegoers of their wallets. Ray, Joe and the girls, however, had backed mainly losers, with money borrowed from Titch. This they were highly unlikely to repay.

On Saturday night, when his elders were sitting around at home in a state of amiable stupor, Titch launched a bitter tirade against everyone else. He complained that he'd had two days of hard work and high risk while the rest enjoyed themselves losing his hard-earned gains. Everyone tried to placate him by praising his professional skill, but Titch refused to be mollified. He then turned on Dan and accused him of lying uselessly around while he, Titch, bore the burden of the day. He grew still more bitter when everyone else sprang to Dan's defence.

In the end, Titch turned on Pop and charged him with abusing his position as head of the family. Pop put down his glass and, without any change of expression, strode over to Titch and buffeted him violently on the head. Titch fell, striking his temple on the corner of a low table. He wasn't knocked out, and got up, slowly, wiping blood from his cheek with a filthy handkerchief. He looked murderously around him, swore once with deep feeling, and went from the room.

'Bloody Titch,' remarked Leo casually. No one else took any notice of the incident. Dan had no liking for Titch, yet felt curiously disturbed. Next day Titch was around as usual, still looking sour but saying nothing.

Dan's cold was nothing like so bad as Olive's influenza had been, but was followed by a racking cough. Pop thought this had commercial possibilities. 'Worth a shilling a time, that cough is, in the right place,' he said, but Mam accused him of being heartless, and it was several days before everyone agreed that he was well enough to resume work.

There was then some discussion over what he should do. Pop, Joe and Ray insisted that the city centre hotels were where the money was made, and that Dan should go back to the Royal Britannia. Leo, Mam and the girls maintained that Dan was too nervous and too delicate for such a pitch. Titch preserved a contemptuous silence. In the end Mam and Leo carried the day by reminding the others that Dan had an additional asset in his singing voice that ought not to be wasted.

'Just the thing for the pubs on Friday and Saturday nights,' Leo proclaimed.

Pop resisted at first, but when eventually he came round to the idea he took it up with enthusiasm.

'Let me explain it to you, Danny Boy,' he said. 'To start with, you're not allowed to go *into* any pub, because you're under age. So you have to sing outside. And you have to choose your pub carefully. It's no good going to the rough ones in the Jungle. On Friday nights there's always women outside them, holding their kiddies' hands and trying to get the old man out before he's drunk all his wages. You wouldn't stand a chance. The better-class pubs over Claypits way are best. Catch the fellers in a generous mood while they've still got money on them, and you'll be all right.'

'The Lamb and Flag would be best for a start,' suggested Leo.

'And what have I to sing?' Dan asked.

'Sentimental songs, Danny. "Home Sweet Home" and "Bless This House" and "It's a long, long trail a-winding". And why not sing "Danny Boy", eh, Danny Boy?' Pop roared with laughter at this witticism.

Next Friday he and Leo took Dan to the Lamb and Flag, which was only half a mile away. They put his cap on the ground, with a few coins in it to set an example, and went into the pub, leaving Dan to practise his art outside. He had little success until closing-time, when an appreciative knot of men gathered around, listening. Pop and Leo were prominent among them, cheering each song and calling for more. Before they dispersed, a shower of coins fell into the cap. The total was just over ten shillings: not nearly as good as at the Royal Britannia, but for much less of an ordeal.

On the way home, Pop and Leo sang 'Danny Boy' raucously at the tops of their voices, concluding in a soulful bawl: 'Oh Danny Boy, oh Danny Boy, we love you so!'

In the three weeks that followed, Dan sang outside most of the pubs in the Claypits area. He had particular success with a temperance song, learned at the Chapel Sunday School, which began, 'Oh Father, dear Father, come home with me now!' This appeal, plaintively delivered, seemed to strike a favourable chord with even the most hardened drinkers, and was well rewarded.

Dan began to take a certain amount of professional pride in his performances. He knew when he was in good voice, and enjoyed the applause and the tribute of freely given pennies. His conscience was eased by a sense that he was earning his keep rather than begging for it. Yet as summer gave way to autumn he began to feel more and more unsettled. Deep in his mind had always been the conviction that some day life would return to normal. He wanted it to happen now.

School had started again, and to his own surprise Dan missed it. Having left the Edge School and never started at Canal Street, Dan seemed to have fallen through the educational net. He was solemnly warned by Pop and

Leo to keep a lookout for policemen and attendance officers who might be inquisitive about a boy at large during school hours.

It became clear that his attempt to reform the Buggy Street family was not succeeding. With the exception of Titch, its members listened tolerantly to his appeals to lead a better life; but they all continued to smoke, drink, swear and indulge in their various illegal activities.

And Dan became aware that his first impression of the family's warmth and solidarity was not quite accurate. The trouble with Titch was not the only strain or stress. Squabbles broke out from time to time between the two girls. There was subdued, and occasionally open, hostility between Ray and Joe, each of whom regarded the other as unduly sharp. Joe accused Ray of bringing off a lucrative car deal and pocketing the money for himself. Ray countercharged that Joe had salted away some big winnings at cards. Pop investigated, and announced more in sorrow than anger that there was truth in both charges. He appealed eloquently for higher moral standards.

Pop had other problems. A deal which he had made for the disposal of certain property, fallen from the back of a lorry, collapsed because the buyer failed to turn up and could not be found. It was always a worry in Pop's line of business when a customer disappeared. He might have been picked up by the police or gone over to some rival outfit. Meanwhile Titch was growing ever more bad-tempered, and was bickering with everyone else.

'Frankly, I'm fed up with the lot of you,' said Mam one evening. 'There's only Dan that isn't a pain in the neck.'

'He's a pain in *mine*!' said Titch.

Next day Titch went to the Picture Palace in Claypits and failed to come in for supper. He was still missing the day after that, and the following morning as well.

'Looks as if Titch has done a bunk,' said Pop at breakfast.

'Good riddance,' said Leo. 'I never did have time for Titch.'

'What do you think he's done?' Dan asked.

'Who knows? Gone it alone, maybe, or joined someone else,' said Leo. 'They come and go, you know. Titch ain't the first to leave, and won't be the last.'

'Still,' said Pop, 'it means loss of income. Titch has talent, there's no denying it, and talent's scarce in this world. Whatever you think of him, he did his share. And things ain't going too well just now, especially with that deal falling through. Fact is, Leo, there's precious little in the kitty.' He turned to Dan. 'It's back to the Royal Britannia for you, young Danny, until things look up a bit. Hard luck, I know, but that's where the money is.'

Panic fluttered Dan's stomach.

'I t-t-told you, I couldn't do it again,' he said. 'I couldn't, I really couldn't.'

''Course you can,' said Pop. 'Come on, Danny, be reasonable. We've took you in, fed you, looked after you. Now we're in a spot of difficulty, you can do something for *us*!'

Dan said no more. He felt some loyalty to Pop, Mam and Leo. But he hated the thought of another night outside the Royal Britannia.

That afternoon he sat by himself on the edge of the landing-stage at the back of the house. Just below his dangling feet was the flat-bottomed boat, covered by a faded green canvas and tied by a length of frayed rope. An early-October sun poured golden globules on the canal's dark surface. It was a fine day, but there was a nip in the air. Winter was coming and he must find his place. And it wasn't here.

He jumped as a shadow fell over his shoulder. Ray had

approached silently from the house. Ray had changed his appearance within the past week. He was at present clean-shaven and had dyed his hair blond.

'You look thoughtful, Danny,' he said. 'Penny for 'em.'

'N-n-nothing,' said Dan. He didn't entirely trust Ray.

'You weren't scowling like that at nothing,' Ray said. He seemed about to sit down beside Dan, but contemplated the grimy wooden landing-stage and his own immaculate suit, and thought better of it.

'Let me guess,' he went on. 'You don't belong here, Danny. Never did and never will. What *you* need is a settled life with your own kind of folk.' Ray preened himself a little. 'I understand you, you see. I don't belong here either. You and me, we aren't like Titch or Joe. They're garbage, Danny, that's what they are, garbage. *We're* a different class. You know what *I* should have been? What I'm cut out for by nature?'

Dan shook his head.

'An actor, Danny. In a better world, I'd have gone on the stage. I could have played in *Hamlet* or *Charley's Aunt* or anything you care to mention.'

'W-w-why didn't you, then?'

'No influence, Danny. No education. I never had a chance. And it's an overcrowded profession anyway. But you got to admit, I have the looks for it.'

Dan agreed that Ray had the looks for it.

'I'm realistic, Danny, I know it's not for me. But I'm ambitious, I'm not staying in the Jungle. When I've got some capital, I'll go into the straight motor trade. Mark my words, before this century's out all sorts of ordinary people'll have cars; they'll think no more about it than if they were wheelbarrows. Those of us that get in soon enough will make our fortunes. As for you, Danny, let me give you some advice. There's been a bit of trouble at Bank House lately, and there could be more. I think you

147

should sort out your family problems and get out of here.'

'That's easier said than done,' said Dan.

'Let's consider it,' said Ray. 'You came down here from the Daisies, didn't you? Your mum's that nice young lady in the photo. But you don't know what's become of her, right?'

Dan admitted it. 'I want to find out,' he said.

'Good. Well, you're talking to the person that can help you. I have a motorcar at present, Danny. It's that dark blue Riley that's standing out in the street.'

'I thought it was maroon.'

'It's dark blue now. And nobody's looking for me. At least, if they are, it's a dark fellow with a moustache they'll be after. I've got an hour to spare before I have to see a customer. Why don't I drive you up to the Daisies, and we'll make some inquiries.'

'I daren't ask at my grandpa's or my auntie's house,' Dan said. 'Or anywhere where they know me. There's been talk of putting me in Broad Street. I don't want that.'

'Don't worry, laddie. You show me where to go and I'll do the talking. People usually tell me things. It's a knack I have, getting 'em to talk. A valuable knack in my line of business, Danny. Leave it to me. I won't let you finish up in Broad Street.'

CHAPTER 25

It was exhilarating to sit beside Ray in the front seat of the Riley as it roared up City Hill, overtaking tramcars and horse-drawn vehicles and frequently touching thirty miles an hour. At Dan's suggestion, Ray parked several streets away from Marigold Grove. Dan gave him directions for finding Grandpa's house, and watched from the car as he headed towards it. It was a long time before Ray reappeared, and when he did so he was grinning ruefully.

'I got into the house all right,' he reported. 'No trouble at all. I told the old biddy I was a long-lost relative of your grandpa's. It went down a treat. She swallowed every word of it. "Call me Hilda," she said within the first five minutes. But she hasn't seen anything of your mum. Doesn't want to, either, she says. She gave her an awful character.'

'She would,' said Dan.

'But I thought you said she didn't like *you*? From what she told me, anyone'd think you were her pet lamb. "He was a dear little feller," she said. "I loved him like my own."'

Ray's mimicry of Hilda's voice was accurate enough to make Dan wince.

'"His mum took him away without a by-your-leave," she told me. "I cried about it for a week." So I said, just out of interest, "Suppose the lad turned up without his mum, would you take him in?"'

'And would she?' Dan asked, not fancying the prospect.

'It made her stop and think, I can tell you. Then she said, "Well, I'm not a blood relation, you know, and I'm over fifty, though I may not look it. And what with his grandpa dying soon after," she said, "I've had a terrible time. And Percy didn't leave me anything to speak of." She was really sorry for herself, Danny. I'd have sympathized with her myself if it hadn't been for the look in her eye. Steely, that's what I'd call it.

'"Anyway," she said, "I really don't see how I could

149

manage it. It'd be up to his Aunt Verity. She's younger than I am, and has a boy of her own already."

'So I said, "What if his auntie wouldn't have him? I suppose it'd be Broad Street for him then?" "That's right," she said. "It's very nice at Broad Street these days, I'm told. Home from home. Of course," she said, "I'd be glad to have him here to tea sometimes."'

Ray was still mimicking Hilda's voice. The last few phrases rang in Dan's ears with dreadful accuracy. Ray noticed his expression and looked at him with concern.

'Don't get upset, lad. Your mum'll still turn up, most likely. And I reckon I ought to speak to your auntie. She might know something that old crow doesn't. If I was your mum I'd be steering clear of *her*, I can tell you.'

'We might as well try my auntie's,' Dan agreed. Ray drove to within a quarter-mile of Aunt Verity's house in Chrysanthemum Avenue. Again he left Dan waiting in the car, and again he seemed to be away a long time.

Dan began to feel bored and also cramped. He got out and walked up and down the pavement for a few minutes. Still Ray didn't come. Then out of the corner of his eye Dan saw a tall, thin figure approaching. A familiar figure: a pale man with a dark beard, carrying a wooden frame. Dan's heart bumped. He remembered Olive's defence of the glazier, but his fear of the man went deeper than Olive's reassurance. He didn't want another encounter with Benjy.

He dodged behind the car and moved around it as the man went past. Benjy didn't seem to see him. Dan got back in the car. Still no Ray. He concentrated his attention on the instrument panel, putting the disturbing thought of Benjy out of his mind. Most of the dials didn't mean much to him, but he could, of course, understand the speedometer. It would read up to sixty miles an hour. Sixty miles an hour – as fast as an express train! How

150

could you possibly travel that fast on an unfenced road? You'd be knocking people over left and right...

'Dan! Dan!' The voice was at the window, right beside his ear. Benjy had seen him after all, and turned back.

'Dan! I want to talk to you! Dan!'

For a moment Dan felt panic. He slid across the seat, meaning to jump out at the other side of the car and run away. Then he took a grip on himself and slid slowly back. The panic had been an instinctive reaction. There was no reason for it. Benjy had never done him any harm. According to Olive, Benjy wouldn't hurt a fly.

He looked, reluctantly, into the man's face. The brown eyes stared eagerly back into his.

'Dan!'

'Yes,' Dan muttered, and looked away again.

'Have you found her, Dan?'

Dan looked towards the glazier, tight-lipped, and slowly shook his head.

'You don't know where she is?'

Benjy was leaning towards him, anxious and insistent, his face only inches away. Dan felt himself to be under pressure. He couldn't bear it. 'N-n-no,' he said; and then, in a bitter little rush of words, 'What's it to do with you?'

'More than you think, Dan. It's important. Specially since your grandpa died. I can't tell you until I find her, and maybe not then. But it matters, lad; you can't imagine how much. And now with Olive, too...'

'Olive!'

'I know you know Olive. You was with her in that attic, like brother and sister. You took care of her. I know. That was well done, Dan ... Where you living now?'

'I have somewhere,' said Dan cautiously.

'You remember, I told you before how I wished I could give you a home. Well, now I may be able to.'

Dan had forgotten this suggestion. It had alarmed him

when first made, and it still seemed baffling. Benjy, the shabby glazier with broken boots, the mender of windows at ninepence a time, as humble as any hawker or odd-job man: how could he provide Dan with a home, and why should he, and what would Grandpa or Mum or any of Dan's relatives have said?

He looked doubtfully into Benjy's face. 'You!' he said, half resenting the idea. And then, suddenly, he felt a change in his feelings about Benjy. The glazier's brown eyes were worried and kind. It came home to Dan at last that Olive had been right. Benjy was a good man, a man who could be liked . . .

At that moment the interruption came. It was Ray, returning, his face furious.

'What you doing here, Shylock?' he demanded. 'Get your hands off my car!'

The glazier straightened up and faced him. 'I was just talking to Dan,' he said mildly.

'You got no business talking to Dan. Dan's in *my* charge, see? He's got nothing to say to you!'

'B-b-but, Ray . . .' Dan began.

'You were holding the door of my car!' Ray accused the glazier. He looked at the spot on the car door as if it might have been contaminated. 'Get away! Go on! Get away with you!'

Benjy stood his ground. 'You don't speak to me like that!' he said.

Ray clenched a fist. For a moment Dan thought he was going to hit the man. But Benjy stepped back, suddenly overcome by coughing. He coughed and coughed, put a white handkerchief to his mouth, and coughed again. Ray made a sound of disgust, stepped into the car, and pressed the self-starter. Then he put his head out of the window.

'Get out of the way!' he yelled. 'Go home and die!'

Benjy, still coughing, withdrew to the pavement. Ray

let in the clutch and drove away, rather fast. Dan was shocked. 'What did you speak to him like that for?' he asked. 'He wasn't doing any harm.'

Ray grinned. His irritation had been short-lived. 'Those fellers need keeping in their place,' he said. 'There's too many sheenies in this city. We'll be overrun by them if we don't watch out. Not that I bear them any malice, mind you. But if I get any nonsense from one of them, I show him whose country it is. That's my policy, Danny Boy.'

Dan had heard such views often enough before. They were common in the city. His own feelings were in turmoil: not from what Ray had said and done but from the shock of that moment when he'd looked into Benjy's face and seen one who cared and might be cared for.

'You never asked how I got on with your auntie,' Ray said. 'Well, I saw her. Got into her house, same as I did with the other one. Told her the same story. If she swaps notes with that Hilda, at least it'll be consistent. Not that there's much love between them these days, I reckon.'

'And she hasn't seen Mum?' Dan asked.

'No, not a sign. I learned something interesting, though. Your mum's fancy-man's come back to the district without her. He's living with his wife and going to Chapel on Sundays, as large as life. No news of where *she* is. But I wouldn't be surprised if she was back in the city too. One of these days we'll find her. Just for the moment, though, it looks like you better stay with *our* family. I hope it holds together long enough, that's all.'

He drew up at the bottom of Hibiscus Street, close to the police station.

'Well, here you are, Danny Boy,' he said. 'You can walk back to Buggy Street from here. I have to see a man about a dog, as the saying goes.' He winked. 'Look after yourself. Don't go talking to Jew-boys.'

'You shouldn't have treated him like that,' Dan said.

CHAPTER 26

Dan set off towards Bank House feeling shaken both by
the encounter with the glazier and by the news that
Uncle Alec was back in the district without Mum. He was
soon to receive a further shock. Ahead of him, walking in
the same direction, was a little squad of half a dozen
policemen.

On instinct, Dan hung back. The squad stopped at the
next corner and went into a huddle. Dan was still
inclined to hang back; he'd been wary of policemen ever
since he ran away. But he told himself that this could
have nothing to do with him; you wouldn't get half a
dozen policemen in a body looking for one missing boy.
All the same, his heart was thumping as he walked past
them.

None of them took the slightest notice. Dan went on
ahead, stepping out as fast as he reasonably could. By the
time he reached Bank House they were well behind. Dan
pushed open the door and went in.

Pop, Mam, Joe and Leo were in the kitchen. They were
drinking tea from thick white mugs and eating pork pies.

'Hello, Dan, love,' said Mam. 'I'm not cooking no tea
today. Having a night off. Grab a pie while there's some
left. They're good, they're from Dobbs's. How did you
get on, up the hill?'

'Oh, all right,' said Dan; and then, 'There's half a
dozen policemen coming along the street.'

'There's *what*?' said Pop. He jumped up, shoving his
chair back. 'Flippin' heck, I knew there was something
wrong, with Parker not turning up and Titch leaving us!'

'They mightn't be coming here, Pop,' said Joe. He stayed where he was and drew calmly on his cigarette.

'You bet they *are*!' said Pop. 'And the stuff's all here that Parker should have took. Somebody's grassed on us. Here, Joe! Leo! Get slinging it out!'

Joe stubbed out the cigarette. Leo took a large bite of pie. They got up, unhurriedly, from the table, just as there was a ring at the doorbell.

'Go on, move!' yelled Pop. 'Joe, shoot that bolt, and then upstairs after me, quick! Leo, out at the back and get the boat untied!'

There was a second ring, followed by a tattoo of fists on the front door.

At last they moved. Dan was shoved on one side by the rush from the kitchen. There was a thudding of feet up the stairs and a sharp sudden draught as the back door flew open. The banging on the front door continued. Dan was alone in the kitchen except for Mam. Huge and calm, she stood up and slowly took her apron off.

'There's stuff up there that oughtn'ter be,' she explained. 'They'll sling it down to Leo. If the back ain't watched, he'll get it away. If it *is* watched, too bad.'

Bang! Bang! Bang! Bang!

'Aren't you going to open up?' Dan asked.

'I ain't in no hurry. Let them hammer away. They'll have a search warrant, no doubt of that, but we don't have to help them. I won't open up till they start breaking the door down.'

Bang! Bang! Bang! Bang!

Mam went into the hallway and called 'All right! Just a sec! I'm coming!'

The banging ceased for a moment. Mam came back into the kitchen.

'Danny,' she said. 'You ain't done nothing. But if you don't want to be picked up, get out the back there with Leo. Go on!'

The banging started again. Mam waddled out into the hallway. 'All right, all right!' she called again. Dan watched from the back, rooted and fascinated. Mam was talking to the police through the closed door now, playing for time, telling them she couldn't shift the bolt, though in fact she wasn't trying.

More banging. Shouts from the men outside, who were getting impatient. Mam made a fierce gesture to Dan to get out.

'What about Pop and Joe?' he asked.

'They're staying. I want them clean, that's all. Now, GET OUT! And lock the back door behind you!'

Dan recovered the power to move. He darted through the back door, halting for a moment to lock it and throw the key in the canal. He heard Mam's voice yelling once more, 'I tell you, I'm coming!' Then he was out on the rickety landing-stage, which shook beneath his feet.

Something flew past his ear.

'Look out, Danny! *Look out!*'

They were throwing things from an upper window to Leo in the flat-bottomed boat. Hairbrushes, candlesticks, a silver-backed looking-glass... objects showered down. The boat rocked perilously as Leo reached out to catch them. Some he missed, and they fell into the canal. A minute later there was a brief thumbs-up sign from Pop, the sash flew down with a bang, and Pop and Joe disappeared from the window.

'C'mon, Danny! Throw me that canvas. Then jump in. Jump *in*!'

Leo was pushing off already. The crumpled green canvas lay on the landing-stage. Dan tipped it down into the boat, then jumped after it, landing on all fours among the assorted loot. The boat was on the move. The walls of Bank House and its two neighbours slid past, then a high fence topped with barbed wire, then a warehouse with all its windows broken. Then a working factory, thrumming away and sending steaming effluent through a pipe into the canal. A high wooden hoarding, a bridge, another factory, and then an open stretch of bank with the row of cottages above which Dan and Olive had lived, a hundred years ago as it now seemed.

Leo rowed on, past the old cottages, under the railway viaduct, and into the maze of quays and inlets that made up the canal company's main basin. In one of the inlets, where rusty rail-tracks ran close alongside, two great barges with tarry wooden hulls were tied up, one behind the other. There was just room between them for the little boat to nose in and insert itself, half hidden, between the bank and the bow of the second barge. Leo tied up to one of the mooring ropes, drew the worn canvas over the contents of the boat, and secured it as best he could in a hurry.

'C'mon!' he said briefly. 'We're off!'

'W-w-what about the stuff?'

'It'll have to take care of itself. We done our best. Come on!'

He had clambered on to one of the barges; now he leaned over and dragged Dan on board. The barge was a few feet out from the bank. Along its side, between hull and superstructure, was a narrow catwalk. They edged along it to a point from which Leo could take a perilous leap ashore. He landed safely and turned to Dan. Dan hesitated, then hurled himself through the air. His front foot landed, but he hadn't the impetus to carry his body on. For a moment he teetered and felt himself falling back; then Leo had grabbed him and they were ashore and running off through the railway sidings.

Dan lost all sense of direction. He merely followed Leo, blundering on over tracks and between empty wagons. Then they were climbing a fence, running along a deserted alleyway and over a footbridge with a narrow black ditch beneath it. Down another passageway, a glint of light on water showed that they were approaching the canal again. They turned aside to edge beneath one of the supports of the railway viaduct.

Beyond it, Leo stopped at last. Both of them were out of breath. They stood, panting. Then Leo said, 'Well, here we are. Can't go back to Buggy Street, that's for sure. What we going to do, Danny? Where'll we spend the night?'

Just in front of them was a little row of four derelict cottages, with its gable end facing the viaduct.

'We'll spend it right here,' said Dan.

CHAPTER 27

Dan was awakened next morning by St Jude's Church clock. It had taken him a long time to get to sleep, and then he'd had wild, confused, alarming dreams, alternating with wakeful spells. Finally, towards dawn, he'd fallen deeply asleep. Now it was eight o'clock or possibly nine; he couldn't be sure he'd counted the strokes correctly.

And here he was, back on his old mattress in the attic above the deserted cottages on the canal bank. For a moment, still half asleep, he expected to find Olive there. Then he remembered. It was Leo who'd come here with him last night. Leo had given up the mattress to him and had slept on the floor, with a folded jacket for pillow. 'This is luxury, Danny Boy,' he'd said; 'I've had it much rougher in my time.'

But he couldn't see Leo now. Dan sat up in panic. 'Leo!' he called. 'Leo!'

There was no reply. Dan peered across into the dim corners of the attic. Leo wasn't there.

Dan dragged his clothes on, dropped down through the trap-door, and inspected the cottages and the out-buildings behind them. Still no Leo. Back in the attic, he picked up his money from the top of the orange-box cupboard where he'd left it last night. There wasn't much – a little heap of silver and copper – but it seemed to be all there. But something was missing that he'd put down beside the money: the photograph of Mum.

Dan winced. The picture, though somewhat battered by now, was still precious. And Leo, for unknown reasons, had always fancied it. Its absence suggested that he wasn't coming back.

Dan was hungry; he hadn't eaten since midday yesterday. He walked along to Dobbs's shop in Hibiscus Street, bought himself a couple of sausage rolls, and stood outside in the street, eating them. Then, cautiously, he made his way along Buggy Street towards Bank House.

There was no sign of police there now, or of anybody else. The front door was splintered, and opened when he pushed it. He went inside, calling the names of the occupants in turn. No response. The house was empty and appeared to have been ransacked. Pieces of furniture stood all over the floors, as if someone had dragged them from the walls to look behind and under them. Drawers had been pulled out and their contents scattered around.

Bank House had always seemed to Dan to be cheerful and fairly well furnished, but in today's cold light all that was left in it looked ugly and worthless. The kitchen table was still littered with remnants of the meal that had been in progress when yesterday's raid began. In the larder were a few scraps of food: a cut loaf, some raw bacon, half a jug of milk and various oddments. Mam had never bought food far ahead. The contents of a sack of potatoes

159

had rolled over the floor. The kitchen range, which Dan had never seen without fire in it, was out. It was hard to believe that only yesterday the house had been warm and throbbing with life.

Dan heard a movement and looked round, startled. In the doorway between hall and kitchen stood Joe: white-faced, black-haired, with the usual cigarette in the corner of his mouth.

'Danny! Danny Boy!' The cigarette wagged gently with his lips. 'Well, well. I'm glad to see you, Danny.'

'Joe! Where were you?'

'Out at the back, Danny, on the landing-stage. Just having a quiet think. Plenty to think about.'

'Where's Mam and Pop?'

'Gone, Danny. They was took in for questioning, of course. Me, too. Three or four hours we spent down there. "Helping with inquiries", they call it. But they was only acting on a tip-off. They didn't have nothing they could charge us with. We'd got all the stuff out of that window before they got inside. They had to let us go in the end.'

'But Mam and Pop didn't come back here?'

'Not on your life, Danny. They wasn't born yesterday. Pop's got a record as long as your arm. He knew the rozzers wouldn't let things drop. They'd be back with something else before long. So as soon as they was released, Pop and Mam lit out of town. They won't be seen round here no more for quite a while.'

'And the others?'

'They've gone, too. With Mam and Pop out of the way, there's nothing to keep them. They'll be thinking it's healthier somewhere else. But, Danny Boy, I got a question to ask *you*. There's one person I don't know about.'

Joe gripped Dan's wrist and put his face close to Dan's.

'Danny, where's Leo? And where's the boat? And where's all that stuff?'

'I don't know where Leo is,' said Dan truthfully. 'I haven't seen him since last night.'

'You've only answered part of my question, Danny. Where's the boat and the stuff?'

Dan hesitated. Joe's grip on his wrist tightened. 'Tell me, Danny. Tell me.'

Dan argued briefly with himself. He didn't want to tell Joe anything. But Joe was stronger than he was. And if he didn't tell Joe, what could he do anyway? He didn't intend to go to the police and invite their interest in himself.

'We tied the boat up in the canal basin,' Dan said reluctantly. 'But I don't know if it's still there. Leo went out before I woke up this morning. He may have moved it.'

Joe swore. 'There's two or three hundred pounds' worth of stuff there,' he said. 'Trust Leo to grab it for himself if he could.' He shook Dan, as if it was his fault. Then he said, 'Well, we'll see about that. Take me to the place, Danny. And' – his voice was very soft – 'don't try to run away. I can run faster than you. Nasty things might happen.'

Dan shuddered. He didn't doubt those last words. He led the way along Bougainvillea Gardens, across Hibiscus Street, down Canal Street, and past the little row of cottages. Instinct told him to say nothing to Joe about these. They followed the towpath under the railway viaduct, where the way was dark and narrow and the black water of the canal was menacingly close. Here Joe suddenly lunged at Dan, pushed him almost over the edge, then, grinning, hauled him back.

'*I* can swim, Danny,' he remarked. 'Can you?'

'N-no.'

'Better behave yourself, then, hadn't you? It's very quiet down here, Danny. Nobody comes. Nobody to rescue you if you fell in.'

Dan shuddered again and walked on, his legs feeling weak. Beyond the viaduct he found the cobbled alley that led away from the towpath. Then came the footbridge, the second passageway, the fence to be climbed, and at the other side of it the rusty web of railway sidings. Dan led Joe across tracks and over quays, unsure of his direction and wondering how Joe would react if he couldn't find the place. But somehow he'd got it right. Rounding the side of a dilapidated warehouse he saw, across a pair of railway lines, the inlet where he and Leo had landed. The two big old barges were tied up exactly as before.

With Joe beside him, Dan looked down from the quay to the little space into which Leo had squeezed the boat the night before.

The boat was gone.

'Th-that's where it was,' he told Joe. 'L-leo must have come for it!'

Joe swore horribly. Then, suspicious again, he asked, 'Are you sure you're telling me the truth, Danny? Because if you're not . . .'

Joe left the sentence unfinished. He was standing on the edge of the quay and gazing round the canal basin, as if in the hope that Leo and the boat might yet come into view. For a moment his back was towards Dan. Without stopping to think, Dan gave him a great shove from behind. Letting out a yell as he went, Joe hurtled into the canal water.

Dan didn't wait to see what happened to him. He'd said he could swim. Dan sped along the quay, round another corner, past another warehouse, across another footbridge. Once again he lost his sense of direction in the maze and didn't know where he was heading; he only knew he must have got a good start on Joe. He couldn't hear any following footsteps. Feeling a stitch in his side, he slowed to a walk. Then he thought of what

Joe might do if he caught him, and forced himself to run again.

The warehouses and quays were behind him now. He was crossing a huge yard. At the far side of it was a high brick wall, much more than head-high, with broken glass along the top of it. He couldn't get over that, and he was now in an exposed position. If Joe came into the yard, he'd see Dan at once. But set into the wall was a pair of great wooden gates that formed the main entrance to the defunct canal company's premises. The gates were closed and solid, but there were stout struts across them.

Dan jumped, clutched, scrambled, fell back, jumped, clutched again and fell back again. It looked as if he couldn't do it. But he leaped desperately up at the gate once more, clutching wildly, and suddenly he'd succeeded and was sitting on top of it. The other side of the gate, fronting on to Slaughter Street, was totally smooth, sheer to the ground: no struts, nothing. It was a long drop. Dan took a deep breath and jumped, bending his knees as he landed. A jarring shock ran through him as his feet hit the pavement, and then he was all in a heap on the ground, breathless and shaken, but safe outside and unhurt.

His head felt very strange, and for a moment his vision was blurred. Then everything came clear. He got to his feet and found himself looking up into the kindly, quizzical face of a policeman: an ordinary, helmeted bobby on the beat.

'You all right, lad?' the policeman asked.

Dan nodded.

'What were you doing in there?'

'N-n-nothing.'

'You're in a mucky state, lad. A shocking state. Where do you live? And why aren't you at school?'

CHAPTER 28

'Brought back by the police!' said Aunt Verity. 'I was never so ashamed in my life! There was this policeman on the front step, standing there for everyone to see, holding this dirty ragged child that I hardly even recognized at first. Found wandering, he said!'

'Dan doesn't seem to be any the worse,' said Uncle Bert.

'His appetite's all right, I can tell you that,' said Aunt Verity. 'You should have seen the way he tucked into my steak pudding. There was hardly any left for Basil.'

'It wouldn't do Basil any harm to eat a bit less for once.'

'I never know whose side you're on, Bert Seddon. Sympathy for everyone except your own family, that's what you have. Think of *me* for a change. How will I ever live it down, a thing like that? Mrs Reddish from just up the street has been round here asking questions already. She didn't get much change out of *me*, I can tell you. But they'll all be talking . . .'

'Let them talk,' said Uncle Bert.

'It's all very well for you. You're out all day, you don't care what the neighbours think. Mind you, I might have guessed this lad would finish up in the hands of the police. I always knew there was bad blood in him. And my own sister's child, at that!'

'My mum hasn't been found then?' Dan asked.

'No, she hasn't. And until today I thought you were with her. I can see she doesn't care any more about you than she does about anyone else. Selfish and irresponsible, that's what Prue always was and still is.'

164

'There, there, don't talk about the lad's mother like that in front of him,' said Uncle Bert.

'It's true, and you know it's true. And I suppose she'll have a new fancy-man by now. She's not with Alec Taylor, anyway. I told you, he's back in the district as large as life, going to Chapel with his wife on Sundays, looking as if butter wouldn't melt in his mouth.'

'Why don't you ask *him* where Prue is?' said Bert.

'Speak to *him*? I wouldn't sully my lips. I've asked at the store where she used to work, though, and they don't know anything. Not that I care, mind you. Prue's no sister of mine, not after what she's done. I want nothing more to do with her. And as for this lad, you know where he belongs? Broad Street!'

Dan's heart bumped at the dreaded words.

'Come now, Verity,' said Uncle Bert. 'You know that won't be necessary. There's plenty of room for Dan here.'

'Corrupting our own boy!'

'Basil's no angel, I can tell you. And listen, Verity, don't frighten the lad with talking about Broad Street. We'll have him, of course we'll have him. You wouldn't put your own flesh and blood into the children's home!'

'How do you know I wouldn't?'

'Because I know you, that's why.'

Aunt Verity sniffed, then suddenly conceded the point.

'You know me too well, Bert Seddon!' she accused him. 'You know I can't overcome my own good nature. There's plenty that *would* put him in a home, I can tell you. Those that haven't any conscience, those that don't care!' She went on, bitterly, '*They're* all right. The wicked flourish like the green bay-tree. It's the righteous like me that get put on. As for you, Bert, it's all very well being generous, but the cost of keeping him's the least part of it. Who has all the work and the trouble and the worry?

You're quite right, Bert, I'm not the kind of woman who'd fail in her duty to her own kin. The lad can stay and I'll look after him, but he needn't think I want to, because I don't!'

'We could make him more welcome than that,' said Uncle Bert.

'I shall do my best for him,' Aunt Verity said. 'I shall try to bring him up the way he ought to go, though if you ask me it'll be uphill work. And, Daniel, I'm not having any more nonsense. You must promise on the Bible that you'll behave yourself in future.'

'W-w-what if my mum *does* come?' asked Dan.

'If she comes and wants you, she can have you. It's not for me to come between a boy and his mother. But until that day, Dan Lunn – if it ever arrives – you're in my charge and you'll do as I say and not disgrace me any more. You understand?'

Dan said nothing.

'Now I'm going to bring the Bible. You're to make a solemn promise, with your uncle and me as witnesses, and if you were to break it there's Another, besides us, whose anger you'd be bringing down on yourself. And don't you forget it!'

Aunt Verity went to fetch the Bible. Uncle Bert took the opportunity to offer Dan a word of reassurance. 'Your aunt's a good woman,' he said. 'Her bark's worse than her bite. You'll be well cared for. You must look on this as your home and try to feel you belong here.'

'Th-thank you, Uncle Bert,' said Dan. He did his best to produce a smile. But it seemed to him that he'd just been asked to attempt the impossible.

Next morning, ostentatiously, Aunt Verity dropped Dan's clothes into the dustbin. She had put him for the moment into old clothes of Basil's which hung, baggy and grotesque, from his skinny frame. When Basil had

166

gone to school, she took Dan into the city centre on the tram. They went to the biggest firm of outfitters, where Aunt Verity kitted Dan out completely with stout, hard-wearing clothes.

'One thing I will *not* have the neighbours saying,' she told him, 'is that I don't dress you properly.'

As each item was purchased, she repeated its price loudly and indignantly – 'Twenty-five shillings for a raincoat! One-and-eleven for a pair of socks!' – making sure that Dan fully understood the expense he was causing. On the way back, she instructed him at length on the proper care of the clothes and the things he was on no account to do while wearing them. These included most of the things that a boy would normally want to do.

Over tea, Aunt Verity told Basil in the presence of Dan and Uncle Bert that he couldn't have a new jacket just yet because she'd had to spend so much on Dan. Basil was understandably aggrieved, though Uncle Bert said Basil didn't need a new jacket anyway. When Basil got Dan on his own, he said two or three times in a threatening tone, 'You wait!' But it wasn't clear what Dan had to wait for. He recalled his defeat of Basil on a previous occasion, and realized also that in the course of his recent adventures he'd grown tougher and a little taller. He wasn't afraid of Basil now.

'Dan won't be going to school with me, will he?' Basil asked his mother at breakfast the next day. Basil went to Claypits High, which was a private school.

'No, he won't,' Aunt Verity said. 'It's not part of my duty to pay school fees for him. He'll go to Canal Street.'

'Where the Jungle kids go!' said Basil. 'I hope he doesn't *get* things!'

'I shall be going down there with him today,' Aunt Verity said. 'There'll be some explaining to do, I'm afraid. But it's not *my* fault he's missed half a term's schooling. He may as well get started there before the mid-term holiday.'

Aunt Verity took Dan to Canal Street on the tram, but told him that in future he would have to walk, which would do him good. 'And I shall expect you back by half-past four each afternoon. That gives you plenty of time. No dilly-dallying. No fooling around. Remember your promise.' Dan suspected that he would be reminded of his promise frequently.

Aunt Verity spent some little time in private conversation with the deputy headmaster. Then Dan was called in, asked a few questions about his accomplishments, and allotted to a class. 'He'll soon settle down,' the deputy head said to Aunt Verity, who aimed a final barrage of exhortations at Dan and then left with the air of one who had done all that could be expected of her.

Dan took his seat in class among some fifty children, mostly pale and ill-clad. He half expected that his new clothes would attract unwanted attention from the others, but in fact nobody took much interest in him. The teacher himself seemed bored and lethargic. Dan soon came to the conclusion that he could dream his way through school without troubling to pay undue attention.

His second day at Canal Street was the Friday before the mid-term break, and unexpectedly everyone was let out an hour early. Aunt Verity hadn't known about this, and Dan had an hour's freedom. And suddenly it occurred to him that an hour might be enough time in which to go and find out what had happened to Olive.

Through the archway, the Shambles looked just as it had done before. For a moment Dan felt the old timidity. But so much had happened to him in recent weeks that he could push it aside without too much difficulty. It wasn't that he'd stopped being afraid; it was just that he took less notice of his fear.

The same piles of garbage seemed to lie in the passageways; the same mongrel dogs to be snarling at each other. A different woman – tall, gaunt and extremely pregnant – was filling her bucket at the outdoor tap. An alley cat prowled around a dustbin. Dan threaded his way through the maze to the little dark entry at the end of which was Frank's and Olive's dwelling.

The paintless door was ajar. Dan knocked on it twice, loudly. No reply. He stepped inside. The remains of a meal were on the deal table, with two or three empty beer-bottles. There was a slight, sweet smell of decay.

It now occurred to Dan that Olive might be at school. Children from this side of the tracks went to Claypits Elementary, not to Canal Street. Probably they hadn't been let out early. Meanwhile there didn't seem to be anyone at home. He pushed open the remaining doors of the dwelling. Besides the living-room and kitchen, there were two small bedrooms. In one of them was a brokendown brass bedstead; in the other there was only a bedroll on the bare boards. Dirty clothes lay around on the floors of both rooms, and there was a smell of unwashed bodies. It was a sorry contrast to Aunt Verity's spotless house.

Dan was shocked. He'd heard Olive say she tried to keep the place clean, but it didn't look as if any effort had been made recently. He felt uneasy in the empty dwelling, and decided he would hang around outside in the hope of meeting Olive as she came home from school. Cautiously he let himself out, closing the outer door gently behind him. But before he could get out of the narrow entry that connected this dwelling with the street, the way was blocked by two people just coming in.

Dan flattened himself against the wall and hoped they

would pass by. But they didn't. He knew them both. One was big, beefy Frank. The other was Doris, from Bank House. Frank had his arm round Doris and they were laughing together.

'Here. I seen you before, haven't I?' said Frank.

'Why, it's Danny!' said Doris. 'Fancy that! What you doing here, Danny Boy? Oh, Frank, doesn't that appealing look of his melt your insides?'

'It don't melt mine,' grunted Frank. He added, in a heavily indulgent tone, 'You women are all alike. Soppy as hell.' Then he frowned. 'I *know* I seen this lad before, but I can't bring it to mind. No, son, don't try to sneak away. I'm not letting you go till I find out what you're up to. Come inside!'

He propelled Dan into the dwelling. Doris sat down on one of the battered chairs. 'Give us a fag, Frank,' she said; and then, after lighting up, 'Didn't think I'd see you again so soon, Danny Boy. Not after Mam and Pop took their hook and the family broke up. Didn't think I'd see *any* of you again. Thought we was just scattered to the winds, as you might say. Well, now, Danny, tell us what you're after.'

'I c-c-came to look for Olive,' said Dan.

'*That's* it!' said Frank. His brow cleared. 'I remember now. 'Course I do! You was in that attic with our Olive!'

'And you took my money,' said Dan.

'Now, now. None o' that. That's over and done with, see? But what you want our Olive for?'

'I j-j-just wanted to find out how she was.'

'Well, you're too late. She's gone!'

'G-g-gone?'

'That's what I said. Gone.'

'Where's she gone?'

'I don't know where she's gone. I only know who she's gone with.'

170

'And who's that?'

'I don't know why I'm telling you this. It's none of your business. Anyroad, you know that tall Jewish feller, the one that mends winders?'

Dan's heart gave a lurch. 'Yes,' he said.

'*He* took her. Only a few days ago, it was. He said he could give her a home. And seeing I don't need her no more, what with Doug going off on his own and me going to get married...'

'That's right, Danny Boy!' said Doris, beaming. 'Frank's going to get married. To me! C'mon, Danny, congratulate us!'

'B-b-but ...' Dan was bewildered by these rapid developments.

'It's right, lad,' Frank said. 'She's me fiancy. I been hooked at last. Plenty of lasses have tried, but it's Doris that's getting me to the register office!'

'He doesn't mind about me having been on the game – I mean, in the love business,' said Doris. ''Course, I'm giving it up now I'm getting married. I'm not a career-girl really. I'm the domestic type at heart.'

'So, like I say, I don't need Olive no more,' said Frank. 'And when this feller came along, offering her a home, I thought, well, I thought, it's in her own best interests, I won't stand in her way.'

'And is he going to adopt her?'

'How would I know? He didn't tell me what he was going to do. She went with him quite willing.'

'I'm not sure you shoulda done it, Frank,' said Doris thoughtfully. 'There's no telling what a feller might get up to with young girls. And a Jew-boy at that.'

'I've known Benjy for years,' said Frank. 'I don't know nothing against him. I don't know nothing against Jews, for that matter. Most of them what I come across are a sight better than the ones that call them names.' Then a thought occurred to him. 'I knew there was summat

171

else. Of course, that was it! He was asking about this lad, too!'

Dan's heart bumped again.

'That's right!' Frank went on. 'I remember it all now. He was talking about making a home for you and Olive. Said you was like brother and sister. I said, "What's in it for you, Benjy? Or are you barmy, wanting to bring up other folks' kids?" He didn't say anything to that. So I said, "Well, I don't know where the lad is, but if you want Olive you can take her." So he did. That's all I know. And now, I'm thirsty with all that talking. Have we got owt to drink, Doris?'

'We got nowt in bottles. Not till this evening. I'll make you a cup of tea.'

Frank laughed. He was in a good humour. 'Women!' he said. 'You want a drink and they make you a cup of tea. And we aren't even married yet! . . . All right, Doris love, I'll have a cup of tea. Put plenty of sugar in it. You want a cup, lad?'

'No, thank you,' said Dan. 'I'll be going now.'

'All right. Suit yourself. Anyway, if you want to find Olive, find the Jew-boy. That's all I can tell you.'

Dan trudged away towards Aunt Verity's, his free hour spent. He was reflecting that everything had changed. Benjy had seemed to be looking for him. Now he would have to look for Benjy.

CHAPTER 29

'You can come with me tomorrow morning,' Aunt Verity said to Dan over tea. 'I'm going up to Bar Lane cemetery. It'll do you good.'

'Why should a trip to the boneyard do anybody any good?' asked Uncle Bert with his mouth full of baked beans.

'It will make him think of serious matters,' said Aunt Verity. 'He can see his grandpa's grave and ask himself what his dear grandpa would have thought of his recent conduct. And perhaps it will help him to be a better boy.'

'No getting away from old Percy, is there?' said Uncle Bert. 'Even when he's dead.'

'Bert!' Aunt Verity was outraged. 'What an example to set! I take it *you* don't intend to go to Bar Lane tomorrow.'

'No, thank you.'

'And what about you, Basil?'

'I'd have liked to go, Mum, and pay my respects to Grandpa. But I've got so much homework.'

'I'm sure your grandpa wouldn't have expected you to neglect your homework for his sake,' said Aunt Verity. 'He'd have understood. He was always self-sacrificing. Very well, Basil, you can come next time. It will have to be just Dan and me.'

Basil put out his tongue triumphantly at Dan as Aunt Verity left the table. Dan knew Basil wouldn't be doing any homework. But he didn't mind not having Basil's company.

It was crisp and clear next morning as he walked with Aunt Verity up the hill to Bar Lane cemetery. It wasn't far. His aunt was wearing black and carrying a large bunch of chrysanthemums to put on Grandpa's grave. Dan wore his new, and only, suit, and a black tie borrowed from Uncle Bert.

As they arrived at Bar Lane a tramcar drew up and fifteen or twenty people got off, all with the same aim. They trailed in a sombre little group through the cemetery gates. The cemetery was a closely planted forest of stone and marble, stretching up, down and round the hillside. You could measure the length of human memory by the state of the graves. Near the entrance were the oldest graves, going back for eighty years or more, long since forgotten and grown over. Then came more recent ones, forty or thirty or twenty years old, mostly untended, but with an occasional patch that had been cleared and dressed with a few flowers.

At the farther end, to which the visitors made their way, were the most recent graves. The lettering on their headstones was still clean and fresh, and the flowers clustered thickly. And at the farthest point of all, this city of the dead ran out into half-rural territory, where there were lines of mounds too new for headstones, and two or three graves dug but not yet occupied.

The narrow lanes between rows of graves were as numerous as the streets of City Hill. All had names. Grandpa lay in Remembrance Avenue. Aunt Verity, peering through her thick spectacles, had some difficulty in finding the way through the maze, but managed it at last. Grandpa's grave, though one of the newest, had its headstone already in place, for Grandpa had been prepared. Most of the inscription had been carved before he fell ill, and all that had remained for the monumental mason to do was add the year of his death.

Dan and Aunt Verity were still some distance from the grave when Dan saw that there was somebody there already. A small person, with back towards them, wearing a navy-blue coat. The coat was just like Mum's best. The small person must be . . .

Dan broke into a run, shouting 'Mum! Mum!' The person at the grave got up, looked round, and hurried away through the maze. Dan ran after her, still shouting 'Mum! Mum!' An elderly man in black, wearing a bowler hat, seized his arm.

'That's not the way to behave in a place of rest!' the man told him severely.

'I thought I saw my mum!'

174

'You've lost your mother? A big boy your age? You'll soon find her. Take your time about it. Don't make all that noise!'

Dan tried to wrench himself away, but couldn't. Aunt Verity came bustling up, full of apologies.

'Here you are, you see!' the man said. 'Here she is!'

'That's not my mum,' Dan said. 'That's my auntie.'

'I'm sure she'll take care of you.' The man raised his hat to Aunt Verity. Aunt Verity apologized several times more. She took a firm grip on Dan's hand and led him along to the grave.

'But I saw Mum! I'm sure I did! At least, I think I did. It was her or somebody just like her.'

'*I* never saw anybody,' said Aunt Verity.

'But you wouldn't, would you? I mean, your eyesight...'

Aunt Verity didn't like any mention of her poor eyesight.

'I'd have seen your mother,' she said. 'You must have been mistaken. You've always had too much imagination, Dan Lunn. I don't see how your mother could dare to show her face at your grandpa's grave, after what she did to him!'

They stood side by side in front of the grave. The inscription on the headstone reflected Grandpa's quiet confidence. It read:

PERCIVAL HENRY PURVIS
1854–1922
'Blessed are the pure in heart,
for they shall see God.'

The mound before it was immaculately tidy, and there were fresh flowers in a glass jug.

'You see?' Dan said. 'Somebody's been. I bet it was her!'

Aunt Verity wouldn't have that. 'Your grandpa had

many friends and admirers,' she said. 'It doesn't surprise me to find flowers on his grave. It would surprise me more if there *weren't*.' All the same, just in case the flowers were Mum's, she removed them. 'It was your mother's actions and yours,' she explained solemnly to Dan, 'that *brought* your grandpa to this place.'

'B-b-but I thought he had a weak heart.'

'He might have lived for many years. He never recovered from the shock of what Prue did, and then your disappearance. It is sharper than a serpent's tooth, Dan, to have a thankless child.'

Aunt Verity lectured Dan all the way home from the cemetery. She assured him that she had not yet lost all hope for him, and that she would work unsparingly for the improvement of his character. Dan allowed all this to wash over him. He *had* seen Mum. The more he thought about it and recalled that brief image of the small person hurrying from the grave, the more certain he was. And there was one person around who had seen her more recently than anybody else he knew: one person he had to talk to.

'Uncle Alec!' Dan called. 'Uncle Alec!'

After Chapel next morning, the worshippers were straggling homeward. Mr Alec Taylor was among them. Beside him walked his podgy wife, Alice, and his two small, immaculately dressed daughters, Enid and Mavis.

'Uncle Alec!' called Dan again, catching up from behind.

Alec Taylor looked round in irritation. His eyes were instantly wary when he saw Dan. His wife had turned at the same moment, and the two of them looked meaningfully at each other, then turned away again and walked on, trying to take no notice.

'Uncle Alec!' Dan called yet again, desperately.

Several people were looking with interest in his direction, for everyone in the congregation knew about the scandal of Mum and Uncle Alec. Mrs Taylor hissed 'Shhhhhh!' at Dan. But Dan stayed right behind them, still trying to attract Uncle Alec's attention. He had chosen good tactics, though he hadn't been aware of doing so.

'You go on home with the girls!' Alec Taylor told his wife eventually; and he himself dropped back to walk alongside Dan, slowing the pace so that the other worshippers were obliged to move ahead. This they did with obvious reluctance. When he and Dan were some way behind the rest, Alec said crossly, 'Don't call me ''Uncle.'' I'm ''Mr Taylor'' to you.'

'But you *told* me to call you it,' said Dan.

'That was a long time ago. Things are different now. Anyway, what do you want?'

'I want to ask you about my mum.'

They were close to the Edge, on which there was an empty bench. Alec Taylor led the way to it, dusted it with his pocket handkerchief, and sat down carefully. He sighed.

'You haven't much sense of tact, have you?' he said. 'Buttonholing me after Chapel, of all times, with half the congregation watching, and their eyes on stalks!'

'I'm s-s-sorry. I just had to talk to you about my mum. I didn't know how else to do it.'

'I knew that was what you wanted. I expected it. Well, that affair's over. And the less said about it the better. Mrs Taylor wants to put it all in the past. I've come back to her and I'm settling down and behaving myself, see? But the truth is, she's still jealous of your mum. She thinks that if your mum just beckoned with her little finger, I'd be off with her again.'

Dan surveyed Alec Taylor dispassionately. He was a

tallish middle-aged man with a little bristly ginger moustache. His suit was pressed and his shoes were shiny. There was a faint air of the dandy about him. But his hair was receding and he had the beginnings of a paunch. He wasn't all that impressive.

'W-where is she now?' Dan asked.

'I don't know, Dan. Honestly I don't. Maybe it's just as well. When you're older you'll understand these things better. I never meant to take your mum away from you. I was happy enough seeing her once a week. She was a nice change from Mrs Taylor. But your mum got cross with your grandpa and fed up with the way she had to live, and all of a sudden she wanted to break loose. It didn't work, Dan. And now I've lost out, all ways. Here I am, back with Mrs Taylor, and I don't have the consolation I used to have. And the whole neighbourhood whispering!'

Dan felt bitter. 'My mum ran away from *me* as well as Grandpa,' he said. 'She didn't care!'

'No, lad, that's not right. She did care. She missed you. That's one reason why it all went wrong.'

'She could have found me,' said Dan. 'She could find me now, if she wanted. I think I saw her at Bar Lane cemetery yesterday.'

'You may have done. She's in the city somewhere. I don't know where. We agreed we'd go our separate ways. Your mum won't show her face to your aunt or her stepmother, because of the disgrace. It's worse for a woman than a man, of course. But she wants you back, when she's put a new home together. She did tell me that.'

'Is she . . . with somebody else?'

'Not that I know of, lad. She was going to look for work. But I wouldn't care to say there isn't somebody she *wants* to be with.'

Alec Taylor sighed.

'You may as well know, son. You're growing up fast, you got to live in the world as it is. Fact is, your mum was in love long before she met me, before she got married, before everything. And deep down in her she still is, with the same man. That's the other reason why it didn't work, her and me. I was better than nothing, maybe, but I wasn't the right one for her, and we both knew it.'

Dan's heart lurched. 'Who is it?' he demanded.

'I don't know, Dan. If I did, I'd tell you. All I know is that your grandpa wouldn't let her marry him. They had to promise never to speak to each other again while he was alive. Nor ever to tell you the truth.'

'You mean . . .' Dan said, and paused, overwhelmed by the size of the thought. 'This man could be my dad. My real dad.'

Alec Taylor looked him in the eye.

'Could be, son,' he said. 'Could be. And now, you'll have to excuse me. I mustn't be late for Sunday dinner. Mrs Taylor has the whip hand just now. I got to be on best behaviour all the time, or it all starts up again. She's never going to let me forget.'

CHAPTER 30

Dan sat for half an hour on the bench on the narrow grassy strip they called the Edge. In front of him the ground fell away sharply to form the Cleft. Opposite was the district of Claypits, packed like City Hill with hundreds and hundreds of houses, puffing out smoke into the grey autumn air.

Dan sat and thought, and went on thinking.

According to Uncle Alec, Mum had been in love with someone whom Grandpa wouldn't let her marry.

But Grandpa had let her marry Jack Lunn, had almost forced her to do so. Jack Lunn, who drank and lost jobs and wandered off for months on end. Surely there was no one more undesirable than Jack. If he was within the pale, who could be beyond it?

Slowly, light dawned on Dan.

The most important thing in Grandpa's life was religion, of his own severe and narrow kind. Grandpa had detested all Catholics. And there were those he had detested even more than Catholics: those whom he believed to have crucified his Saviour.

With virulent passion, Grandpa had hated Jews.

CHAPTER 31

Dan and Uncle Bert arrived home at the same moment, equally late for Sunday dinner. Aunt Verity deduced from Uncle Bert's breath that he'd been to the pub. This earned him an enormous scolding, while Dan got away almost unscathed. Afterwards, Aunt Verity clattered dishes angrily in the kitchen. Uncle Bert, about to settle down for an afternoon snooze over the newspaper, remembered something and pushed a crumpled envelope into Dan's hand.

'A red-haired lad came up to me,' he said. 'Asked if I was your uncle. When I said I was, he gave me this for you. What is it, Dan? A cheque for a thousand pounds?'

Dan didn't answer. He was tearing the envelope open. The note inside it was laboriously written in pencil:

Dear Dan

Sorry about the stuff, but am leaving town to join Mam and Pop and we need money.

Also I have kept your photo as a ~~sov suv~~ souvenir. I would like to find a young lady like your mum the right age for me some day. Well, no harm in hoping.

Goodbye from
Your friend
Leo.

P.S. I have seen someone just like her but older, serving in the tea-room in City Park.

CHAPTER 32

City Park wasn't far away at all: just opposite the cemetery, in fact. Dan had been within a stone's throw of it yesterday morning. It was small and desolate and not much used at this time of year. A bandstand stood empty in the centre; round the edges were flowerbeds, but the flowers were finished and the beds drooped with little dark wallflower-plants, holding on for next spring. In one corner a single massive beech-tree proclaimed the autumn, spreading the October gold of its branches against a pewter sky. In the opposite corner was the tea-room. It wasn't much more than a shack. Daylight was failing, the last customers had left, and it was about to close.

And she was there, the one remaining member of staff, wiping down the tables. She saw him, knew him, and dropped her gaze. Dan was ashamed that his mother could not look him in the eye.

She put down the cloth. Dan put his arms round her and she wept, briefly. Then she took a tiny white handkerchief from her sleeve, wiped her eyes, and gave him a watery smile.

'You're taller than I am now,' she said.

'You left me,' said Dan. 'You never came back.'

His mother said, 'I'm working, Dan. I have a room. I'll save till I can get a home together. Then I want you, if you'll come. But till then you're better off with your auntie. Perhaps you always will be.'

'And what about my dad? My real dad? You never told me who he was.'

'I couldn't, Danny. I swore to your grandpa I never would. Never, never, never, that's what he said. I've done so many wicked things, I couldn't break my Bible oath as well. And it wouldn't be good for you to know.'

Dan said, 'You don't have to break your Bible oath. You don't have to tell me. I know already. And it *is* good for me to know. It's Benjy, isn't it?'

She nodded. She was weeping again.

'I think you should go to him now,' Dan said quietly.

'But how could Benjy still want me? After Alec Taylor, and all the disgrace?'

'He *does* still want you. I know he does.'

'You sound so grown-up, Dan. You shouldn't be troubling yourself with things like this. You're only a boy. You should go back to your auntie's and put it all out of your mind.'

'I'm not going to put it all out of my mind,' said Dan. 'I'm going to put it all together.'

CHAPTER 33

Dan felt alive to his fingertips with hope and determination. His quests for a mum and a dad and a home and a family were all now leading him the same way. What he had to do was to find the glazier. And Benjy was always around on City Hill.

Monday, the day of the mid-term break, was also the day of the Canal Street school outing. Parents who could afford it paid two shillings towards the cost of a day trip to the nearest bit of seaside. Dan decided that as a new pupil he could fail to turn up for the outing and not be missed. He could also borrow Aunt Verity's two shillings. It hadn't yet occurred to her to give him any pocket-money.

He began his search early. He asked about Benjy at shops all over the Hill; he even stopped housewives in the street. He half expected to see the man walking the streets with his wooden frame. But success didn't come as easily as he'd hoped. Everyone knew the glazier, but nobody knew where he lived. Nobody knew of any friend or relation he might have. He was always alone. No one had seen him in the last few days. Several people remarked that he'd been looking ill, but nobody knew more than that.

Dan refused to be discouraged. He was going to win through. In mid-morning a vital hint led him to the workshop in Back Violet Street of the Clear View Glass Company, proprietors H. and F. Hindle. Great vertical racks stood against the inside walls of the shop, and when Dan went in one of the Mr Hindles was cutting panes of glass on a huge felt-topped table. He was a solid, slow-moving man with an extremely deliberate manner, and as he worked he discussed the weather in great detail with a customer who seemed equally unhurried. Some time passed before he could give his attention to Dan.

'Poor old Benjy,' he said at last in reply to Dan's inquiry. 'I always felt sorry for him. Cast off by his own family and never found no other. He didn't make much of a living, you know. Couldn't get a proper job, being the wrong race as you might say. But he was a decent, honest man, and I ought to know, I've dealt with him long enough. Folk talk as if Jews was all rich, but there's plenty of poor ones in this city. I've known Benjy on winter days with his arm so stiff from carrying glass that he couldn't move it till he was thawed out. And that cough of his . . .'

'But is he still around?' Dan asked.

'Not regular. He ain't mending no more winders. Benjy's gone.'

'Gone!'

'He's left the district, lad. He had to. It was Horace's doing. That's my brother. He listened to Benjy coughing in here one day, cough, cough, cough, and he says to me, quiet like, "That cough's going to carry him off," he says. And Benjy says, "What are you whispering about?" And Horace says, "It's time you saw a doctor about your cough." So Benjy says, "Where would I get the money to pay a doctor?" And Horace says, "Well, you been coming here a long time, Benjy. I reckon we owe you a bit of discount," and gives him half a crown. It costs half a crown to see a doctor these days, you know. Some of 'em charge more.'

A second Mr Hindle appeared from the back of the shop. Dan blinked, for he was an exact replica of the first. They were obviously identical twins. The pair of them, stout and dignified, stood side by side behind the counter, surveying Dan solemnly.

'I was just telling this lad,' said the first Mr Hindle, 'how you persuaded Benjy to see a doctor.'

'I did that, Fred,' agreed the second Mr Hindle. He looked gravely at Dan. 'Next day,' he went on, 'in comes Benjy for ninepence worth of twenty-four-ounce glass. So I says to him, "Well, Benjy, what did the doctor say?" And Benjy says, "It was a waste of your money, Horace. He told me to get out into the country if I wanted to stay alive. Seems I got a spot of something on the lung."

'"So what are you going to do about it?" says I. "What *can* I do about it?" says Benjy. "He might as well tell me to live in the South of France."'

'And that's where *I* came in, lad,' said Fred. 'For it just happens I have a pal whose cousin knows somebody whose husband's boss has a row of cottages at Upper-shaw, fifteen miles out of town. And there was one to let at three shillings a week, and a job to go with it as night-watchman at the mill there. So we got old Benjy all fixed up. 'Course, we lost ourselves a customer by doing it, but we don't grudge Benjy a bit of luck, do we, Horace?'

'I reckon he deserved it,' said Horace. 'The funny thing is, although he was so much alone, what Benjy really wanted was a family. Anyway, lad, why the interest? What's Benjy to you?'

'I thought *I* might have a family connection with him.'

'You?' Fred studied his face. 'You Jewish, then? I wouldn't have thought so, not at first sight. Would you, Horace?'

'Oh, I don't know,' said Horace thoughtfully. 'Maybe I would. And look at his eyes. Don't you think his eyes is like Benjy's?'

Dan gulped. The ghosts of Grandpa's prejudices rose up before him. Was it really possible that he himself . . . ?

185

The brothers were looking at him with growing interest. 'Hey!' said Fred. 'Hey, you aren't by any chance the lad that was living in that old attic in Gumble's Yard, are you?'

Dan nodded.

'With a little lass called Olive?'

'That's right.'

'Hear that, Horace?' said Fred. 'It's him.' The pair of them beamed across the counter at Dan. 'You can't be wanting Benjy more than he wants you, I can tell you. And there's someone else he's looking for, too.'

'I know. My mum. And I know where she is.'

The brothers were delighted. 'There you are!' said Horace triumphantly. 'I see how it is now! Old Benjy's reserved, like; he don't tell you everything. But I can put two and two together as well as the next man!'

'Benjy's ships is coming home,' said Fred. 'And he's waited long enough. If ever a man deserved a bit of luck...'

'Well, now,' said Horace, 'what we going to do about it? Benjy don't have no telephone in that cottage at Uppershaw. But he comes into town maybe once, maybe twice a week, searching. Being as he's on nights, he can get away in the daytime, but he don't like to leave the kiddie on her own too often. Now when he's in town, Benjy always calls in here...'

'So if the lad gives us his address ...' said Fred.

Dan's face fell. Horace read his thoughts. 'He don't want to *wait*,' he told Fred. ''Course he don't. He wants things to happen *now*. Well, we know where Benjy lives. The lad can get on a train to Uppershaw and go find him. Sooner the better.'

'You got any money, lad?' asked Fred.

'I've two shillings.'

'That all? It mightn't be enough. Here's two more.'

'And here's another two,' added Horace. 'That'll be

plenty. Off you go, now. There's a train to Uppershaw every half-hour from Peterloo Station. Number Two, Ross Mill Cottages, that's where you'll find Benjy. And the little lass too, most likely, seeing it's mid-term. And you'll be welcome there, I can tell you.'

'Here, hold on a minute!' said Fred. 'What if Benjy comes in here today? He might be on his way now. Then they'll miss each other.'

Horace scratched his head.

'It doesn't matter if he misses *me*,' said Dan. 'But he's got to find *her*. Lend me a pencil.'

He took from his pocket the note he'd received from Leo. Carefully and heavily, he crossed out everything except the postscript. He also deleted the first nine words of the postscript and put two others in their place. When he'd finished, the message read simply:

She is serving in the tea-room at City Park.

'There,' said Dan. 'If Benjy comes in today, just give him that.'

CHAPTER 34

The steam train chuffed and chuntered its way out of Peterloo Station, through the marshalling yards, across the viaduct that Dan had seen so many times from below, and out through acres of humble, grimy housing. It stopped twice at suburban stations, then settled itself to the long, slow haul up Rawdale.

Rawdale. There was nothing green about this valley. It was lined with factories, mills, warehouses and engineering works, through which a thick dark scummy river threaded its sluggish way. Uppershaw was the train's sixth stop: an old stone village that had come sprawling down the hillside to meet the industrial jumble in the valley-bottom.

Dan gave up his ticket, watched the train chug away, and got directions from the solitary porter for finding the way to Ross Mill Cottages. It was a steady trudge uphill. The weather was cold and grey, and there was a slight chilly breeze. Dan found himself at the same time eager and alarmed at the thought of the reunion ahead. What happened when you met, for the first time as your father, a man you'd known all your life as a strange and rather frightening figure?

He didn't know. But he was prepared. A dad was a dad, just like a mum was a mum. And at least there was nothing alarming about the thought of meeting Olive. Dan trudged on.

The tidemark of industrial development was halfway up the side of the valley. Above it, the country changed. Drystone walls scored lines across the landscape; sheep grazed; small hill-farms were scattered around, and on top of everything were dark, sweeping moors. Dan shivered and followed the road: up and round, round and up.

Ross Mill was an old water-mill, long since replaced by a steam-powered one down the valley. Ross Mill Cottages were a row of perhaps a dozen small dwellings built for its workers. They were reached by a dirt track and stood close to a little overgrown quarry from which most likely their stone had come.

There were no roses round the doors, no picturesque thatch, no tidy gardens full of flowers, no soft pastoral scenery. This was a spartan setting: bleak, rugged, primitive. Yet these were cottages, and in spite of all the industry sprawling in full view far below, this was country. And the wind blew fresh. For a man with a spot of something on his lung, it would be healthier than city streets.

The second house in the row had been painted recently. Smoke rose from its chimney. Its front step had been scoured. Dan knew immediately that it was the one. He stood in front of it, rooted by fear and shyness, collecting the courage to lift its black iron knocker.

But he didn't have to. The door was flung wide open. She threw her arms round his neck. Olive.

She released him in a moment, laughing at his puzzlement.

'I saw you coming!' she said. 'I watched you from the window. You can see right down the hillside from here!' And then, 'You're home, Danny! It's your home! Come in!'

There was a fire. The room was shabby, and everything looked second-hand. But it was clean, warm, welcoming.

'Where's . . .?' he began.

'Benjy? He's gone into town, Danny, looking. Looking for you. And here you are. How's that for a surprise? He'll come back tired, and here you'll be, waiting!'

'Will he go to the glass place?'

'Oh, yes. He'll go there first, probably. They're his friends. He don't have many friends, Danny, but he has *them*.'

'Then he'll find my mum. I expect he'll bring her here.'

'That'll be nice.' Olive sounded matter-of-fact about it. 'I wouldn't mind having a mum. And it'll make Benjy happy. He's good to me, Dan, I can't tell you how good he is, but he's not been happy. Now p'raps he'll have all he needs.'

'What if *she* doesn't like it?' said Dan, struck by an awkward thought.

'She'll like being with Benjy. 'Course she will. Who wouldn't?'

Dan remembered Alec Taylor's words: 'She was in love long before she met me. And deep down in her she still is, with the same man.'

'Are you thinking she mightn't like *me*?' Olive asked. 'Cheek! She'll like me all right. *You* like me, don't you? Well, then, so will she. What you worrying about?'

'I'm not worrying,' said Dan; and he wasn't. After a minute he asked, 'What time did Benjy leave home?'

Olive told him. They worked out together the time it was likely to take to get from Uppershaw to Peterloo Station, from the station to the glass company, from the glass company to City Park, from City Park back to Peterloo and from Peterloo to Uppershaw. They came to the conclusion that there must still be at least two hours to wait.

They sat opposite each other at a table in the window, from which they could keep the hillside in view. Olive told Dan that country life was a bit funny but the village school was nice. Dan told Olive about his adventures in Buggy Street and afterwards. They seemed to have an endless amount to talk about. Dan never stammered once. Olive mended the fire and later, seated at the window, began to make suggestions about a meal. Then she jumped up.

'They're coming!' she cried, and was out of the room and away through the front door in a matter of seconds.

Dan followed as far as the cottage doorway. Yes, he could see them, far down the lane, a tall figure and a small one, side by side. Olive was flying down the hill towards them. Just for a moment he hesitated. Could everything really work out? There were so many complications: Mum was married, Benjy's health was in doubt, Aunt Verity would have plenty to say. There'd be fuss and palaver. But in the end those who didn't want him would give him up to those who did.

Olive had reached the couple below and was embracing them vigorously, then dancing between them and holding hands with both as they resumed their way uphill. There was something familiar about the picture. Suddenly it clicked into focus with the one that had been in Dan's mind, all that long time ago. The imagined family: the real dad, the small sister, and Mum, all united and affectionate.

Along with that memory, absurdly, Grandpa's storybooks came into his mind. The stories, with their discoveries of rich relations and their triumphs over wrongdoing, hadn't borne much resemblance to what actually happened to him. But there was one thing about all those stories that was true of real life as well. Things could come right. You could have a happy ending.

He ran down the hillside to meet his parents.